$\mathcal{D}$edication

Henry Esten Burmeister-Brown was born on
October 9, 1995,
six pounds, thirteen ounces,
and healthy in every way.

So many of you have sent tender good wishes.
Thank you from the bottom of our hearts
for giving him such a welcome
to the world.

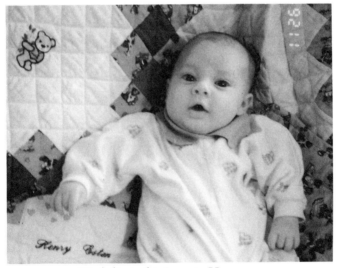

We dedicate this issue to Henry,
and to every child
everywhere.
May they be heaped with love always.

Susan Burmeister-Brown   Linda Davis

ONTENTS

EDITORS
Susan Burmeister-Brown
Linda Davies

CONSULTING EDITORS
Annie Callan
Dave Chipps

COPY EDITOR & PROOFREADER
Scott Allie

TYPESETTING & LAYOUT
Florence McMullen

COVER ILLUSTRATOR
Jane Zwinger

STORY ILLUSTRATOR
Jon Leon

FINAL-PAGE ILLUSTRATOR
Bernard Mulligan, Republic of Ireland

PUBLISHED QUARTERLY
in spring, summer, fall, and winter by
Glimmer Train Press, Inc.
812 SW Washington Street, Suite 1205
Portland, Oregon 97205-3216 U.S.A.
Telephone: 503/221-0836
Facsimile: 503/221-0837

PRINTED IN U.S.A.

Glimmer Train (ISSN #1055-7520), registered in U.S. Patent and Trademark Office, is published quarterly, $29 per year in the U.S., by Glimmer Train Press, Inc., Suite 1205, 812 SW Washington, Portland, OR 97205. Second-class postage paid at Portland, OR, and additional mailing offices. POSTMASTER: Send address changes to Glimmer Train Press, Inc., Suite 1205, 812 SW Washington, Portland, OR 97205.

ISSN # 1055-7520, ISBN # 1-880966-17-4, CPDA BIPAD # 79021

DISTRIBUTION: Bookstores can purchase *Glimmer Train Stories* through these distributors:
Anderson News Co., 6016 Brookvale Ln., #151, Knoxville, TN 37919
Baker & Taylor, 652 East Main St., Bridgewater, NJ 08807
Bernhard DeBoer, Inc., 113 E. Centre St., Nutley, NJ 07110
Bookpeople, 7900 Edgewater Dr., Oakland, CA 94621
Ingram Periodicals, 1226 Heil Quaker Blvd., LaVergne, TN 37086
IPD, 674 Via de la Valle, #204, Solana Beach, CA 92075
Pacific Pipeline, 8030 S. 228th St., Kent, WA 98032
Ubiquity, 607 Degraw St., Brooklyn, NY 11217
SUBSCRIPTION SVCS: EBSCO, Faxon, READMORE

Subscription rates: One year, $29 within the U.S. (Visa/MC/check).
Airmail to Canada, $39; outside North America, $49.
Payable by Visa/MC or check for U.S. dollars drawn on a U.S. bank.

Attention short-story writers: We pay $500 for first publication and onetime anthology rights. Please include a self-addressed, sufficiently stamped envelope with your submission. **Send manuscripts in January, April, July, and October.** *Send a SASE for guidelines, which will include information on our Short-Story Award for New Writers.*

ONTENTS

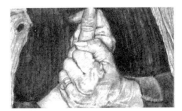

It's ready to fly!
160

Robert Cohen

Circa 1961: my stance.

Novels written by Robert Cohen include *The Organ Builder* and *The Here and Now*. The latter was published January 1996 by Scribner.

Cohen teaches creative writing at Harvard University.

ROBERT COHEN

The Boys at Night

*T*he baby arrived in summer. The baby: that was how we referred to her, no name, no gender, just the baby, as if her infancy was not a passing condition but a defining one. In a sense, it was. But then we were all in need of some defining that summer. I was fourteen, though I acted younger; Paulie was eleven, but seemed much older; and my parents, those large, irritable people who sat across the table at dinner, were hovering around forty. Whatever *that* meant.

One thing it seemed to mean was a difficult pregnancy. During the last trimester my mother, suffering complications, was ordered by her doctor to relax in bed. Now I should explain that my mother was famously high-strung; asking her to relax, in bed or anywhere else, was a little like prescribing Valium to a coat-hanger. Impulsive, nervous-fingered, kinky hair springing gid-dily from her head, even in sleep she was never still but lay coiled on her side, shuddering involuntarily, a tall, toppled animal assaulted by dreams. For the baby's sake, however, she tried. From May to July, she confined herself to the bedroom; there she lay buttressed by pillows, cooled by fans and ice water, not so much relaxed as temporarily arrested—reading, distractedly switching channels on the television, consuming yogurt by the quart, and fretting about things beyond my comprehension.

Outside, the world went about its usual business. Big cars swooshed past on their way to the city. Mowers roared; kids splashed in their pools; grackles dive-bombed in the mulberry trees. We could hear it all through the windows. But we did not join in.

After dinner a certain confusion would set in. My father, having eaten almost nothing, would retreat into the long folds of the newspaper; my mother, exempt from her usual duties, would waddle back to bed with a Graham Greene novel and a box of cookies; and Paulie and I would be left to clean up the kitchen, to put away the leftovers and grumble about doing the dishes. I'd grumble too, though the truth was I rather enjoyed doing the dishes. It was a relief to have something small and manageable to do, to lose myself for a while in the warm water, mindless repetition, and lazy fizz of the suds. And boy, did I ever need to lose myself. I was a restless, avid, unfocused kid; nothing would have delighted me more than to have this self of mine turn up missing.

If life, as Mao said, is a permanent revolution, then mine was proving no exception. I had militant hormones and an unsteady constitution. My skin launched bloody insurrections; my voice warbled and cracked; my dreams rumbled from detonating lusts. At school the previous year my grades had gone into free-fall, and my popularity teetered for a while and then followed with a whoosh. Girls with their fine radar veered away. Teachers regarded me with suspicion. Even my guidance counselor was shocked by the abruptness of my descent. I'd better shape up, she had declared with an authoritative wave of my file; I was in danger of "slipping between the cracks."

What cracks? I wanted to ask. But ask who? My friends were busy or away that summer and my family had for all intents and purposes taken up residence on Saturn. Occasionally in the evenings, when my mother was in bed and the kitchen table wiped clean, my father and Paulie and I would leave the house and take long, aimless walks by the river—walks whose sole purpose, so far as I could tell, was to allow my father room and time to smoke—and I would think, yes, now, okay, let's *go*. But where? In the failing light my father looked distant and tired; deep lines of effort squirmed on his brow. Here he was, out with his two sons; what now? Or was he thinking about us at all?

The truth is that even on his best days, my father's manner was halting, indeterminate, as if beset by inner fog. As a young man he had done his share of running around in New York—where he'd tried, for a while anyway, to become a poet—but over the years he had acquired some new, sober weight that kept him in place. Perhaps I was that weight. Me and Paulie. If so, we did not want to think about it. The heat was making us sullen and balky; in our ears the mosquitoes whined like kazoos. Besides, all of us were tense that summer, irritable, dreaming of other places. Not just him.

My mother's frustrations were easier to read. Before being ordered to relax, she'd worked in the city as a paralegal. She was generally acknowledged as a hot number at the firm. There were senior partners who claimed she could be judge material if she'd go back to law school and pay her dues. But that adventure had lasted only one semester. "I can't wake up at six, work all day, then come home and read at night," she'd complain. "My eyes hurt." The truth was she had too much vanity and too little patience to sit through classes taught by people her own age and attended by kids in their twenties. Their ambition wearied her. Ultimately she concluded that it was enough to know she *could* have been a star; she did not actually have to go out and become one.

On weekends, however, a less compromising side of her would emerge. She'd sleep late, throw around money, treat herself to matinees. My father rarely joined her in these indulgences—he'd be grading papers or working on the lawn— but for a time, a long time, I did. We'd catch every movie that came to town, and, as she watched, my mother would lick popcorn butter off her fingers and let out small, complicated sighs, and I would feel implicated in her desires in a way that was illicit and thrilling. At the same time I'd catch myself and wonder if maybe I should be somewhere else, some*one* else, not sitting with my mother in the complicated dark, feeling the weight of her disappointments.

Mama's boy, Paulie would say on those occasions—and there were a growing number of these—when he was feeling vengeful. He knew it; I knew it. It would not have surprised me if in the whirling privacy of her thoughts my mother had had occasion to use the phrase herself. As for my father, he must have seen it too, though he was either too generous or too preoccupied to let on. He never said anything about it, not even that disastrous night at the bowling alley, when he probably should have. But then none of us were ourselves that night—no one but the baby. And that was the problem.

I should not blame too much on the baby. As I said, things were already going very badly before she arrived.

Take football.

My body, that fickle and clumsy machine, had recently on its own authority taken on two extra inches of height and ten extra pounds of bulk—at the same time jettisoning my brain, it appeared, altogether—thus emboldening me to go out for junior varsity football. There were no cuts in football; anyone who wanted to could be on the team if they stuck it out. I figured I could stick it out. Even the brutal regimen of double practice sessions that began in early July and ran to the end of August, when the season itself commenced—even that didn't bother me. Desperate to realign myself, to trade in my free agency for a uniform, an identity, I figured I could stick out practically anything.

But in the end it was only my wrist I stuck out. And it came back broken.

We were doing tackle drills at the time. We did them every day. Tackles, as the coaches had ample occasion to remind us, were a fundamental part of the football business, and it was necessary to practice them often, like piano scales, that they might be executed in a certain consistent way. Tackles were to be quick, low, and crisp. There was a sound one listened for, a brief crunch of impact followed by the slow crumple and hiss of a body folding upon itself. This, they said, was the sound of execution.

I was a competent but ungifted football player, a fact that was becoming increasingly clear to me, though it was not yet solidly established, I don't think, in the minds of the coaches. To compensate I had to get by on smarts and craft: on *education*. I listened hard, steeped myself in the fundamentals, drew x's and o's on a chalkboard in my head. I listened particularly hard that day. The coaches were not happy with our execution, they said. They went over the whole tackle idea one more time, wondering, with some justification, if we were too stupid to get it. Later, when one of the guards forgot to pull on a sweep, I had a good shot at Kevin Kelly, the starting halfback, as he made his turn upfield. I decided to show off how well I'd been listening. Sure enough, I hit him quick and low and crisp at the knees. Sure enough, he went down as if shot.

The coaches were delighted; they summoned everyone over to watch me execute the tackle again. Kevin dusted himself off. Coolly impassive, he took another handoff, slanting outside tackle. I moved sideways in pursuit, holding my upper body straight the way I'd been taught, crossing my legs like a crab. About five yards downfield, our paths intersected. Kevin saw me coming and lowered his head. I could see in his eyes that he was getting a little tired of tackle drills at this point. A little tired of execution.

I did not hit him quite so low or so crisp as before, but I got

enough of him—or was it the other way around?—that we both
went down in a heap. When Kevin, attempting to rise, shifted
his weight and rolled heavily toward me, there was a snap. That
was when I discovered, at the bottom of the heap, my left arm.
The snap itself did not sound like a big snap. Not a snap that
could actually *affect* anything, I thought. Not in the long run, not
in my *life*.

But it was. My wrist was broken: compound fracture. The
doctor said three months at least. Kevin, shaken up, sat out a few
plays, drank some Gatorade, and went on to a fine season.

Well, my father said on the drive home, a little adversity, you
know, is a test of character. That might not be a bad thing.

I was to learn a great deal about my threshold for adversity in
the weeks that followed. Unfortunately most of what I learned
was how little adversity I'd previously encountered, and how
enervating a thing adversity really was, and how great was my
desire to live a life free of it.

Now that I was home all day, there were no checks whatever
on my sense of boredom and superfluity. My friends were out
of town or on the team or otherwise engaged, and Paulie—we
were, after all, close in our way—was busy with the Science
Club and the assortment of weird, intricate projects that had
occupied his attention for as long as I could remember. In the
past I had never been particularly curious about how my brother
spent his time, but now, as I performed my sullen rounds
through the quiet house, I'd catch myself loitering at his
bedroom door, watching him conduct chemistry experiments,
or take notes for one of his screenplays, or tinker with a
homemade radio, or any of the other activities that kept him so
wonderfully insulated from the common weather. Once I
looked in and found him running through some Marx Brothers
routines with Harold and Steve, his only friends. I was certain
they'd invite me to join them, but they didn't. So much for
fraternity.

All of which is to say that from my point of view, it was almost a relief when the baby arrived.

My mother went into the hospital on a Friday morning, and did not come out until Tuesday night. Aunt Millie drove up from Baltimore to stay with us. Millie was a big, high-hipped redhead with a grudge against half the world—the male half. Her mistreatment by this half had come very early and then matured over the years, and by this point it was something of a trademark complaint, preeminent among a host of others, such as the cost of henna, the barbarism of the Arabs, and the stinginess of the J.C. Penney Corporation, where she was employed as a buyer. She had a habit of talking very quickly, often to herself, and drinking water all the time, and whether these were due to some medication she took or merely neurotic by-products of loneliness, I had no idea. Genetics, that merciless lottery, had awarded my mother the good looks and the romantic disposition, leaving Millie the big hips, the shrewd temper, and the majority of the domestic skills. I was not blind to her heroism under the circumstances. The sight of Millie basting a chicken for our dinner, her apron (brought up from Baltimore) tied neatly at her neck, her plucked eyebrows knitted in concentration, nearly broke my heart. She'd turn out prodigious meals we didn't like and sit there with me and Paulie, clacking her nails on the table as she waited for us to eat. Everything's going to be fine, was her mantra for the weekend.

"Why can't we go see her?" asked Paulie.

"Your mother's very tired. She wants to rest for a while first."

Paulie looked skeptical. He'd been reading up on the labor process and was entertaining suspicions. "The cord might've gotten trapped around the neck," he whispered later, as we brushed our teeth. "That cuts off the oxygen."

"Shut up, Paulie."

"That's what you always say. 'Shut up, Paulie.' That's your answer for everything."

"Just shut up."

Possibly I had a greater influence on Paulie than I thought, because in the weeks that followed he hardly spoke at all. But then everyone was a little distracted, because of the baby.

At first they didn't tell us anything was wrong, and we didn't ask. True, there was a flatness to the skull, and the eyes seemed wrong somehow, but I was not looking closely—not at her, not at anything. My mind was a dull tool. If my father was right and adversity was a test of character, then already I could feel myself failing; closing up, turning in, shutting down. All I knew was that my wrist had betrayed me at a decisive moment, and as a result I would not be playing football that autumn, let alone making All-County, let alone proceeding to a brilliant professional career and the adoration of millions. None of that was going to happen. Knowing this, all of my ambitions for myself did a quick 180; suddenly I burned to be away, far away, college maybe, so that the rest of my life, my *alternative* life, whatever it was, could begin.

Oh, and I knew one more thing. I knew my parents were on the outs. And it had something to do with that little creature they'd brought back from the hospital.

I remember one night in particular. It was six o'clock or so. Millie was chattering away like gunfire on the phone and wrestling with a pot roast in the oven. My mother came into the dining room and fell into a chair, still chubby from being pregnant and bleary-eyed from no sleep. Her bathrobe was loose; through the folds I had a glimpse of the forking, intricate blue veins in her stomach. The sight unnerved me. I looked around for the baby but she was asleep in the bassinet—which, I had come to understand, was as much as one could hope for from babies.

Meanwhile, Paulie was leafing through a magazine and nibbling a cracker. As a rule he had deplorable eating habits, my brother; he got away with it because of his ethereal thinness and pallor, his air of preoccupation with things higher than food. The less you seem to care about something, the more you get away with, in my experience.

Outside it was still light.

My father came in then and Paulie didn't look up when he sat down. "Put the magazine away," my father said. "We're having dinner."

"So?"

"So put the magazine down."

Very deliberately, Paulie folded up the magazine and placed it under his chair. It was quiet. Either Millie had hung up the phone or else she was actually listening to someone else talk for a change. Or perhaps she was listening to us. Paulie's eyes were now fixed on his plate, where the magazine had been, as if he were still reading. "What were you reading about, anyway?" I asked, just to get him talking.

"Yes," said my mother, looking up at us for the first time. "Tell us, Paul. Tell us what's going on out there in the world."

"How should I know?" He snapped it out bitterly, as if we'd insulted him.

"You're the one with the magazine, schmuck," I reminded him.

"So?"

"Both of you lower your voices," said my father. "You'll wake the baby."

At approximately this point Millie waltzed in, bearing the enormous brisket in its covered pot. "I hope everybody's hungry," she said brightly.

"Oh, Christ," my father muttered under his breath.

Quickly, unsure if Millie heard him, I said, "I'm starved."

For a while, after she'd dished out the food, Millie seemed to lose all sense of purpose. Fluttering back and forth, she wiped her hands on her apron, checked her watch, opened the oven, peered in, then closed it again. We were all waiting for her to sit down. Finally she came hovering to a rest behind Paulie and leaned so close their cheeks met. "Paul, honey, eat a little, okay? You're turning into a twig."

"I'm not a twig," said my brother, the literalist.

"Just a little, hon. Just a bite." I could see Millie trying to catch my mother's eye, exchange a meaningful look, conspire together in this house of obstinate men. But my mother was looking out the window rather obstinately herself. "You sure?"

Paulie shook his head.

Millie gave up. "These boys," she sighed, affectionately mussing Paulie's hair.

"They're good kids," said my father.

"Oh, they're treasures. Darlings. Sometimes when I look at them and see them all grown up like this I think, oh, how they'll turn out, and I just know they can handle ... I mean if they have t—"

"Millie," my father said quietly.

For some reason, this one rather benign mention of her name drove all the blood from Millie's face. A silence followed. In its tenor and duration it was unlike all the other silences we had endured of late, and I began to wonder, as it stretched on and on, just what this handling we were capable of might be.

Finally Paulie seized his chance. "Can I be excused?"

My father said no. My mother said okay. They spoke at the same time, then stopped and gazed across the table curiously, as if each trusted the other must be right and was now waiting to hear why.

Steam was rising from the brisket; it made my face feel hot, crowded. "I've got stuff to do too," I said. Though I didn't.

Finally my father let out his breath—apparently he'd been holding it—and looked down into the messy crevice of his potato. "You're both excused. Go have a good time." He didn't sound terribly optimistic about our chances, however.

After we left, the adults remained at the table, talking quietly among themselves about God alone knows what, and the next morning Millie packed up her apron and went home. I rode with her to the train. Choking on her perfume, I hugged her good-bye—more tightly, I think, than either of us expected—while my father, a few feet away, dug into his pockets to tip the redcap. "Be good, honey. And listen," she said, "whatever happens, you really shouldn't blame him, you know." *Good how?* I wanted to ask. *Blame who? For what?* But there was no time for explanations; my father was already coming over to kiss Millie on the cheek. Afterward he lingered a moment, whispering something into her hairdo. Millie nodded. "I know that," she said, her eyes unnaturally bright. "I know."

Yes, I was sorry to see Millie go; that's how bad things were getting. The house was airless and cramped and smelled of diapers, formula, unwashed dishes. Sitting through meals was a trial. It reminded me of the few times I'd attempted, in the interests of family unity, to watch *Masterpiece Theatre* with my parents. You kept hoping for some action, or a laugh, some form of liveliness or spontaneity, but forget it. That was what our meals were like.

Around this time summer session at the college let out, so my father now had a lot of time on his hands, too. It's a curious thing being between semesters, between years of school, between past and future—*between the cracks*—and I don't know that any of us handled it very well, but it seemed to me that my father did not handle it at all. He retreated to his study, where he read novels, drank iced coffee, and listened to jazz. He seemed to be looking for excuses to get away from the baby. But who could blame him? I was eager to get away myself.

One day when it was very hot we did get away, down the shore to Asbury Park. When we arrived the surf was low and inviting, and it cost me a great deal not to immerse myself, though by wrapping a plastic bag around my cast I was able to wade out a little. Still, I was happy to be there and tried to make the best of things. Paulie, wearing a T-shirt to avoid sunburn, spent the entire day reading on the blanket. He did not care for the beach. Neither did my father, for that matter. He swam for a while and then when neither of us would join him he built a sand castle, by himself, fussing over it for close to an hour. He looked hurt that we weren't more impressed. The effort seemed to exhaust him. For lunch he gave us a ten-dollar bill and let us buy as much junk food as we wanted. Then he lay down for a nap.

Later that afternoon I took a walk by myself, picking up rocks and throwing them dopily at the waves, as if it mattered, as if anyone, myself included, cared whether I hit them or not. It occurred to me that I missed my mother terribly, a thought that shamed me. I really was a mama's boy, it seemed. What would that mean?

I turned around and headed back. When I was still some distance away I happened to look up and see, through the waving screen of humanity, my father. He was sitting on the blanket where I had left him, staring vacantly ahead—arms hugging his knees, fisherman's cap pulled down low over his eyes—and as I watched he did a wondrous, awful thing. He picked his nose. He did it savagely, making a pincer of two long fingers, digging away like a miner. While I was at it, I also noticed that his chin was weak, his doughy pancake of a chest had no hair, and his flesh pooled at the hips into droopy love-handles. It did not seem possible that this man I called my father was forty years old. Because there was something about him that was not solidly formed, he looked, without his shirt and tie, like another person—like a big, gawky, thoughtful kid. Like *me*. Abruptly I wanted to run off and hide, that I might no longer have to approach him this way. But it was too late; he was right in front of me, and I was helpless to change course.

"Hi," I said, and sat down on the blanket beside him. Paulie grunted but did not look up.

"Hey, pal," he said.

"I was just off wandering, you know. Down the beach."

"How was it?"

"Okay."

Just then a girl of about sixteen floated past us in a bikini. I watched her for a second, dully thoughtful, and then I saw that my father was following her with his eyes too, and I felt, among all the other things I felt that day, a flicker of hatred for us both.

"What's her name going to be?" I asked.

"Hmm?"

"The baby. You guys going to name her or what?"

He considered his knees for a moment, as if the answer might well be inscribed upon them.

"I just thought, you know, it's been a couple weeks now."

"Has it? Has it really?"

"Sure."

"Yes, you're right," he said hollowly. "But let's talk about it later, okay? With your mother. Let's talk about it later with her."

That night they told us about the baby. It was after the dishes were cleared but before dessert, a time I normally enjoyed because it was so unhurried, the day fading to a blur but the evening hanging, suspended, just before us. They told us that the baby had Down's, and that this was a very serious condition, so serious that for the good of the family they had decided it was unfair to try to raise her, and that there was a good chance that by the time school started she would no longer be living with us but at a place set up to deal with Down's children, to give them a good—that is, a *better*—life, though she would always be our sister and we would visit her at every opportunity and remain close to her somehow, always. All together, it required about ten minutes to explain the complexities.

When they were finished, they asked us for our opinions—my parents were like that—and I spoke up right away, saying that it didn't matter to me very much one way or the other, I just wanted everyone to be happy. Paulie waited until they asked him specifically, and then he said he felt the same way. My mother's eyes in the dusk were luminous and still. She had slowed down enormously since the baby; she was no longer the same restless person. Even her hair had calmed down, flattened out. She reached for us with her long fingers and pulled us close, murmuring how much she loved us, would always love us. Normally my mother's embraces were fitful, rapid, arrhythmic; but this one went on and on. She remained on her knees before us, perhaps begging, perhaps praying, perhaps only tired, while my father, who'd been standing a step or two behind her, waiting, gave up and went to the stove, where he stood peering down into an empty coffee filter. I could see the impatience in his shoulders, his eagerness for Paulie and me to go to bed, for all the explaining to be over. It was perfectly obvious, I thought, who wanted what, and whose will had prevailed.

The next day my mother put on her good sundress, left the baby with my father, and spent the afternoon driving around to institutions. She was gone for several hours. When she came back she was very tired. I asked her how it went and she gave a kind of low, dirty laugh I had never heard from her before. Then she went in to take a shower.

She followed the same schedule three days in a row. None of us offered to go along, and she never offered to take us. The fourth afternoon, however, she was late getting started. None of her clothes seemed to fit right; she kept changing her mind and going back to her closet to start over. I was just hanging around, watching. I must have been feeling particularly aimless that day, because I asked, when she was finally dressed, if she wanted company.

She frowned. "Sure you want to, kiddo?"

"Sure. Why not?"

"Well, school starts next week, you know."

"So what?"

"So maybe you should take it easy. You know, enjoy your freedom."

I shrugged. By now it was obvious, to me anyway, that freedom was wasted on me. I wasn't good at it. I couldn't execute. Freedom was just another crack I was slipping through. "I don't mind," I said.

That day we drove forty miles to Nutley to check out a home. No doubt it was a perfectly average home of that type, no better or worse than most, and yet immediately upon entering I felt I had walked into one of my own bad dreams. The floor had a sickly sheen, the walls were dull white, the corridors were silent, and every adult that went by seemed to be fighting the urge to break into a trot, hurrying to complete some errand or other, following a schedule I would never understand. I wanted to get out of there fast. But my mother was taking her time. She went from room to room, looking things over and asking questions, and then when the tour was over she embarked on a long, leisurely conversation with the woman in the administrative office.

I sat out in the corridor on a plastic chair, waiting to leave.

There were some bulletin boards on the opposite wall to which pictures had been thumbtacked. They were landscapes of a sort. Each one seemed designed to show off the entire spectrum of colors found within a Crayola box: there were blue mountains, yellow lakes, black trees, purple houses, orange fields. Having Down's, I thought, must be like a drug trip. Not that I had ever actually *taken* a drug trip, of course, but I had gleaned from my more adventurous friends that there was something wonderfully vivid and strange about the colors one saw when one was, as they put it, "fucked up." Then I recalled the drawings my mother kept in her bottom desk drawer, pictures Paulie and I had drawn when we were very young, when we'd write our own birthday cards and color them in. Perhaps it was just being young that made it so difficult to see things as they really were.

On our way out, some of the older kids waved at us; others just watched with vague, indifferent stares.

"So what do you think?" my mother asked as we climbed into the car.

"Me?" It hadn't occurred to me when I volunteered that my opinion was going to be solicited. Now I cursed myself for not paying better attention while we were in there. "Hell," I said, "*I* don't know."

My mother, frowning, glanced down at the front of her blouse, where moisture stains had appeared as though from invisible wounds. "They seemed happy," she said. "It seemed like a good, clean place."

"Right," I said. "It wasn't so bad."

"You should see some of the others. It would be pretty educational, I'll tell you that." She took a deep breath and revved the engine. "Buckle yourself in."

As we backed out of the parking lot, I remembered something, a piece of data I might contribute to the decision-making process. "Those pictures on the bulletin board were pretty cool.

I mean, you don't draw pictures like that when you're miserable."

This sounded rather feeble even to me. Also it did not, after a moment's reflection, seem even remotely true. But my mother smiled. It was the first time I'd seen her smile in some time, and the sight encouraged me. She was bearing up pretty well, I thought. Both of us were. We were good and resilient people, and our lives, all present evidence to the contrary, were going to turn out just fine.

"Let's go home, kiddo. Let's go make some spaghetti."

That night we made spaghetti and meatballs. We made garlic bread. We made German chocolate cake for dessert. We made all this food and then as usual nobody but me ate it. My mother was still in a good mood, chatting about little things, people she knew, stories in the paper, movies that she wanted to see, and if there was anything forced or ungenuine about her that night I failed to notice. The baby was asleep in the back bedroom, so for the moment it was the four of us again. I was eating a little; Paulie looked dreamy and irritable; my father had his head bent so far I could see through his hair to his scalp. And then my mother, still chirping away, tried to tell a joke she had heard, and when she arrived at the punch line my father lifted his head for the first time all evening and stared at her in wonder. It was as if even after all these years he could not believe how beautiful she was, and how lucky he was to be married to her.

But what he said was, "Please stop."

At once her face went white, and her lower lip began to tremble. "*You* stop," she said.

"Fine," he said, pushing back his chair. "*I'll* stop. Okay?"

Nobody answered him. It wasn't okay. Whatever okay was, this couldn't possibly be it. But who was going to tell him?

"Great," he said. "So let's go." Standing, he looked around and clapped his hands together. "Who wants to go?"

"Where?" I asked.

"Wherever you want. I don't care. Putt–putt golf."

"No way." I held up my cast.

"Okay, a movie then. What's at the Fox?"

"It's lousy. I saw it."

"Well, what about bowling? You always liked bowling."

This was a fairly bizarre suggestion, coming from my father. He hated bowling. When he had to drive me to league on Saturday morning, he'd remain in the car with his coat on, smoking and correcting papers until I was finished.

"*I'll* go," said Paulie, helping himself to some of the coconut I'd picked off my cake.

I snickered. "You never bowled a game in your life, squirt."

"So what? Mr. Jackson says I have a lot of athletic potential."

"*You?*"

"Sure. I just need to develop it, he says."

"Paulie," I said before I could stop myself, "a *vegetable* has more athletic potential than you."

It would be impossible to overstate how poorly this remark went over at our dinner table that evening. Everyone just stared at me with their mouths open, waiting for me to disappear.

"Okay." I threw my napkin down. "Let's go bowling."

We were halfway to the door when it occurred to me that my mother had not yet weighed in on the bowling question. I turned to look at her.

"Go," she said, and gestured toward the dirty dishes on the table, urgent business that couldn't wait. "Enjoy yourselves."

"Okay," said my father quickly. "I guess it's boys night out."

The night was warm, starless, but there were presentiments of autumn in the breeze. We drove to the bowling alley with the windows down, all of us in the front seat, the radio tuned to the slow, syrupy classical music my father preferred when he was driving. I draped my left arm over the top of the seat, behind Paulie; from time to time the road vibrations made his hair brush against my cast, but if he noticed he did not complain.

There were only three or four cars in the parking lot.

As soon as we stepped inside, the cold air rushed up to greet us, and everything about the place, the hollow thunder of the pins, the girlish squeal of shoes on the polished floor, conspired to draw us in. There was a gaudy new carpet in the lobby, and a separate room for video games in the back. The man at the register was also new. He looked about thirty, and was built on the same scale as the football coaches at school, thick arms and a squat, bulldog neck. A small television was set above the counter. Even as he came forward to deal with us he continued to watch it out of the corner of his eye. Slow night.

"Excuse me," said my father. "We're going to need some shoes."

Grudgingly, the man handed us our shoes and a blank score sheet.

"Which lane?" asked my father, confused.

"Look on the sheet," the man said.

"Why can't you just tell me?"

"Hey, Dad," I said. "Come on. Look, it's right here."

But my father did not move right away. He was looking at the man's back as if it had been inscribed with a line of bad poetry. A muscle worked in his jaw.

"Come on," I said. It had already registered in my stomach that something was off, and that maybe the thing to do was go back home and help my mother with the dishes. But possibly this was just a reflex talking, the mama's boy in me. Paulie was already marching off looking for a ball, shoes slung over his shoulder, so I followed along. My father followed too.

We bowled. Did we bowl! I don't know what came over us that night, but I must have had four or five strikes in the first game alone, and my father—my father was a revelation. He'd been a miler back in high school and had long, powerful legs, and when he swung his hips and let fly, the ball spun and arced down the lane with terrifying velocity. He did not seem to hate bowling at all; perhaps what he had hated, those Saturday mornings, was *not* bowling. In the first five frames he made two spares and two strikes. And that was before he warmed up. On the second strike he pumped his fist and let out a yell—we all did—and then tried to hide his face from us to conceal his grin of satisfaction. We saw it anyway.

Meanwhile Paulie was plugging away, doing his best to bear up under all our coaching. He had neither form nor force, yet most of the time he managed to hit something, and one time he got lucky and pulled off a spare on a tricky seven-ten split. "Cut it out," he complained, as we pounded him on the back. "I'm terrible. I keep missing all those pins."

My father took the opportunity to remind him about Rome not being built in a day, and suggested he relax. Paulie nodded somberly, then two frames later, made another tough spare. This time I was not so certain it was luck.

We bowled three games and there was no stopping us. In the fourth we began to play around, try jazzy approaches to the lane, make cocky little bets. We were so involved that we did not notice the place emptying out, or the lights clicking off in the neighboring alleys. But then I looked at the clock—it was five to eleven—and suddenly I was aware of the surrounding darkness, of Paulie's high voice echoing through the cavernous room. "I think they're closing," I said.

My father was waiting for his ball to come up. "What round are we on?"

"Sixth."

He considered. "What about it, Paul? Want to finish this game, or call it a night?"

"I don't think there's time," I said.

Paulie drew himself up straight. "If we started," he said, "we should finish."

We played out the game. Then we changed back to our sneakers, gathered up our things, and headed toward the front desk.

When we laid our shoes on the counter, the clerk looked at them as if he had never seen bowling shoes before. It was the same man from before. His eyes were even smaller, bluer, and harder; the television in the corner was off. I knew he'd been wanting to close up for a while and blamed us for being slow.

As I say, I knew it. Exactly what planet my father and brother were on was anyone's guess. Even now they were still joking around, comparing scores, promising rematches. I had to nudge my father just to get him to pay. And then I saw him reach for his checkbook, and I knew we were in for it.

"We don't take checks," the man said through his teeth. He waited until my father had finished signing it to tell us.

"Fine, you don't take checks. Here—," my father, still making a joke out of it, took out his wallet, "—look, no problem. I'll give you the cash I have. I'm a little short... three twenty-five, three... okay, I owe you four-and-a-half bucks. Call it five. I'll drop it in the mail tomorrow."

The bulldog just shook his head. He had a kind of nasty gravity that seemed to emanate from his chest and exert itself upon us all. I felt my own head begin to shake in time with his.

"All right then. Why don't you just take my check and we can all go home."

"We don't want your fucking check. I just told you."

"Watch your language, please," my father said heatedly.

"Fuck you."

I heard Paulie draw a breath. The hairs on the back of my neck began to tingle.

"Look, I'll say whatever the fuck I want. You've got no fucking consideration, playing all night when I'm trying to close. Now you can't pay. What are you people trying to pull?"

There was something in "you people" that sent what was happening out of the realm of the personal and made me conscious, as I rarely was in those days, of the curliness of our hair, the size of our noses. The man took a step toward my father, and my father, thin hands trembling, took a step toward him. They were going to fight. It did not seem possible. They were going to fight, and my father—there was little doubt of this— was going to lose, and there was nothing to be done to stop it. Meanwhile Paulie was wobbling beside me, miserably staring at the television; perhaps he was waiting for it to come on again and envelop us in its familiar, perfect glow. But we were out here now, in the accidental world. Out here things built one upon the other with a kind of dumb, brutish, oceanic logic, and no sooner had you put one mess behind you than another loomed in front, and somehow this logic dictated that we must watch our father get beat up by some asshole in a bowling alley for no particular reason. And then in the sickness of that moment I flashed on the baby, lying in the crib at home with her slanty eyes and her flat nose and her lousy, accidental future; and all the rages of the summer massed inside me and toppled like a wave.

I had a flicker of sympathy for my father before I stepped forward and did what I did.

"Get away from me! Get away from me goddamn you!"

According to Paulie, who is not entirely to be trusted in the matter, I was screaming so insanely he could hardly make out the words, and thus wasn't certain who I meant to get away from whom, exactly. Somehow I managed to wedge myself between the two men. Rather than push against the bulldog—who cared about *him?*—I turned and pushed against my father instead, pushed hard. Burying my face in his neck, heaving up from below as I'd learned in football, I moved him away from the counter and a couple grudging steps in the direction of the doorway. "Okay, okay," he said. *"Okay—"* My successful show of force, my execution, and his lack of resistance to it, was such a gratifying surprise that I kept pushing even when we were at the door, Paulie trailing anxiously behind us, even when we were out on the sidewalk that led to the parking lot, even when we were only a few short yards from the car. I would have pushed him the entire way home had he let me. But suddenly my father stiffened. As though waking from some protracted dream, he shook his long head, and a red light dawned in his eyes, and he pushed me back. He did not seem quite so skinny and kidlike to me now, but heavy, immovable. He pushed me, and I pushed him, and then he stopped pushing and grabbed me in a bearhug, pulling me tight against his hard, prominent ribs, shaking me until my eyes blurred. I almost let go then. I was almost overcome by the immediacy of him, the rankness of his sweat, the proximity of his organs below his clothes—I could feel an artery pounding away at me—and a terrible sound I could hear, though I don't think he could, deep in his throat: an uncomprehending cry. Nonetheless I held on. I had a host of grudges to fuel me. If I'd been angered by his weakness, I was angered too by his strength, a strength I'd misread, I now realized, as I'd misread so many other things that summer. My lungs were empty, my breath was raw, but I held on, and locked in our wordless embrace we thrashed and bumped against the car like an enraged two-headed moth, not really getting any-where—for my part, I was no longer trying to—but as if under the grip of some awful species compulsion. At last he grew cunning, and reared up trickily from the hips; clearing some space for himself, he got one hand free, and lifted it high as though to swat me—

That was when he faltered. Perhaps his hand remembered that it was full of the same blood as my own; perhaps it was the pressure of this knowledge that caused it to hang a moment, half-closed, half-open, in midair. Who knew? Who cared? Unfortunately for him, I had slipped sentiment's leash. Almost without thinking—though not quite, not quite without think-ing—I gave him one of my quick sideways hop-steps, raised my cast, and brought it down hard on the side of his head.

He let go of me then.

He did not fall, but stumbled back against the front fender, where he remained in a hunch, trying to catch his breath. Where had it gone?

As for me, I backed away. The punch I had thrown, if that's what it was, had not satisfied me entirely; I still felt myself capable of throwing more. I went over to the passenger's-side door and jerked it open, prepared to punch that too if necessary. Then, immediately upon sitting down, all my strength deserted me. I leaned my head against the seat and closed my eyes. In the distance I could hear cars swooshing by on the parkway. It seemed to me I could taste their exhaust in my mouth.

At last my father got up, climbed stiffly into the driver's seat, and lit a cigarette. "Where's your brother?" he asked wearily, looking around.

I nodded toward the sidewalk, where Paulie was marching back and forth, petulantly kicking gravel with his sneakers. He knew we were waiting, of course, but I suppose he too wished to register his unhappiness that night. My father did not appear to mind the wait. He sat there, smoking. In the glow of the streetlamp his hands were like X rays. He could not keep them still.

Suddenly I had an idea.

"You're the one, aren't you? You're the one that wants to keep her."

He didn't say anything. I was remembering Millie's good-bye: Don't blame *him*.

"Look, just tell me. It doesn't matter; it won't change anything. I just want to know."

"Know what?" He turned to look at me, his mouth twisted, contorted; he might even have been crying a little. "Know what?"

"You know," I said vaguely. "Everything."

He laughed. The sound was private and bitter and even a little dirty, in the same way my mother's had been that first day back from seeing institutions. Not knowing, it seemed, was rather like freedom: large but not infinite, and taken the right way, kind of fun. One should enjoy it while it lasted.

My father was through with me for now, so I turned to watch my brother through the windshield. Hands jammed into his pockets, he was slouching moodily up and down the sidewalk. It used to cheer me up sometimes to consider how different we were, Paulie and I, how glad I was to be me and not him. But right now I did not feel that way. Right now I was less certain of how and where to draw the lines between people, less certain there were lines to be drawn. In a week, school would start, and the uncertainty, I knew, would only accelerate. And more after that. And more after that. Soon I too would endure crises of decision that were inscrutable from a distance and perhaps even to me, and no one could tell me all I needed to know to avert them.

Finally Paulie came over, opened the door, and slid into the back seat. He was very tired, he said, and wanted to go home.

My father remained quiet, lost in thought.

"Hey," said Paulie, leaning between us. "What're we *waiting* for?"

"Shut up," I said. "We'll be there soon."

WAYNE DYER
Psychologist, writer

$\mathcal{I}$nterview
by Linda Davies

Wayne Dyer

**Wayne Dyer earned his doctorate
in counseling psychology from Wayne
State University and has since written
fourteen books, including the bestselling
Your Erroneous Zones. Dyer has been
called one of the original self-help gurus.
He's currently promoting his newest book,
Your Sacred Self (Harper-Collins).
Dyer lives in Florida with his wife and
children.**

DYER: Who's in the picture over there?
DAVIES: *That guy on the wall? It's just a picture my sister found in a
thrift shop. We're both kind of fond of old pictures. But it always startles
me that wonderful pictures like that are available in thrift shops. I think,
My God—*

Why doesn't somebody treasure this?

*Exactly! When you look through old family photos, is there one person
to whom you feel most drawn?*

My brother. My older brother. I'm the youngest. We went
through the orphanage and the foster homes together. My father
left when we were really young. I was an infant; I don't
remember my father at all. He was an alcoholic and went to

prison and our mother was in her early twenties. My brother is a good person, but he was really scarred by all that.

At what age would you have liked to have found a book like the one you've just written [Your Sacred Self]?

I think these are things that most of us know, but I don't think I myself would have been ready—I have eight children and some of them are much more ready for these kinds of things than others of them are—I had to go through the stages, to this stage. Even ten years ago, I didn't know this. In fact, I don't even know that I know it now. This was almost what I would call automatic writing. It just came to me. I just sat down and surrendered and let it come. I almost see myself as a messenger rather than as an author.

You'll probably reread this yourself then.

I reread all my stuff; I even reread *Your Erroneous Zones* and apply it. One of the great teachers of my life is Carl Jung. Carl Jung wrote a book in 1951, when I was eleven years old, called *Modern Man in Search of a Soul*. It's a really powerful book. I read it when I was a teenager. In it, he said there are four stages that adults go through. And I had to go through all of these stages. The lowest stage he called the Age of the Athlete, which is disappointing to a lot of people, but he wasn't putting down athletes, or athletics even. He was saying this is when our primary identification is with that which is physical, with our bodies; how strong they are, how fast they can run, how much they can lift, how pretty they are—that becomes our focal point. A lot of people, he says, stay at this level in their lives. The next stage is called the Warrior, where you take your physicalness out into the world and you conquer. To compare, to achieve, to collect, to set goals, to meet your own quotas. For a lot of people, that's their life. In fact, most people stay there. If you get past that, the third stage is called the Statesman, where you stop asking, *What are my quotas?* and ask, *What are yours? How may I serve?* and your focus shifts away from your bottom line and your goals and what you can achieve for yourself, and on to making the world a better place, serving other people, seeing the unfolding of God in others, and so on. And then the highest stage he said you can get to, he called the Spiritualist. This is when you really know that you're none of the previous things. You're not even a human being having a spiritual experience, it's the other way around; you're a spiritual being having a human experience. It is this stage of being a spiritual self where you stop focusing on what you observe and what you notice, and you shift into becoming the observer or the noticer. When they asked Buddha how to define what is real, he said, *That is real which never changes.* And that's the only thing that is real. So when you start looking at yourself and asking what part of you meets that definition, it's certainly not your thoughts and it's not your body or your career or any of those things, because those things are always undergoing changes. But the part that's noticing all of this is changeless; it's the eternal part of ourselves. I think what happens is that we get stuck under the spell of matter, so we think that what we call matter is all there is, and we lose sight of the fact that the cause of everything in the physical dimension including ourselves is not in the physical domain. You didn't decide to need glasses and I didn't decide for my hair to fall out. It's in an unseen dimension. You can't find *Wayneness* in Wayne; you can't find *Lindaness* in Linda. It's in an unseen dimension. It's just happening, you're just noticing it. It's going to do whatever it's going to do and that's true of everything in the physical domain. So we have to learn how to shift into the dimension that is the cause of our physical world and most of us don't know how to do that. I've only recently learned how to do that. And when you can do that, when you can go into that unseen dimension, you can become a manifester in your life, you can manage the coincidences of your life—you can co-create your life. As Christ said, "Even the least among you can do all that I have done and even greater things." We have that capacity, but most of us don't even have a clue. So I don't think this book would have done me any good.

34

I was an Athlete, and I was a Warrior for a long time, and I was a Statesman for a long time. But to understand this unseen dimension that I'm talking about, where you can literally participate in the act of creation yourself and manifest whatever you want—healings, divine relationship, abundance, whatever—become the observer in your life rather than what you observe.

The idea of being the observer is one that I hadn't thought of before, but when I read this book, I did try to step back and look at what my life was doing, what I was doing, and it was interesting to be able to look at it enough to laugh at it before jumping back into it.

It isn't that you can leave it totally, but you can say, *Look, there goes Linda. I'm glad it's not me. Poor Linda, she's such a fool. She thinks all of this is so important.* You can think, *She's so neurotic. It's fun to watch her.* What happens, I think, is that we have to go back and forth between these two dimensions, but after you get into this, it's much more fun being the observer than being that which you observe. It's really cool to be able to go there. Another great teacher in my life was Abraham Maslow, and when I asked him what self-actualization was, he said that all you have to do is become independent of the good opinion of other people and you got it. You got it. Self-actualized people are not attached to the outcome, which is what the *Bhagavad-Gita* teaches: to be detached from the fruits of your labor. They're fearless; they're not concerned whether you like what they say or don't like what they say. They're not inconsiderate. He used to give an example in his classroom, he'd say, *There's a formal party and everybody's dressed up in formal gowns and black ties, and this self-actualized soul shows up in sandals and a T-shirt and a pair of jeans; what does he do?* That would be the question that he'd ask the class. And they'd all study this and they'd say, *Well, he wouldn't pay attention to that; he wouldn't go home to change; he would be unconcerned with that; he would just go on.* And Maslow would say, *None of you got it. You don't get it. The thing is he wouldn't notice.* When you are independent of the good opinion of other people, that's when you're the witness. Because the witness doesn't care.

This woman who used to come to me when I was a therapist was depressed, chronically depressed, and I would say to her, *Is there any part of you that isn't depressed or any time of the day that you're not depressed?* I'm looking for a place to start. Maslow taught me that if you really want to be healthy, you're not motivated on the basis of repairing deficiencies; you're instead motivated on the basis of growth. Where you are is where you've chosen to be and you honor that and accept that. So I wouldn't want this person to think of the thing that is wrong with them. This woman said, *No, I'm always depressed. There's no organ in my body that isn't. I dream depressed and I wake up depressed.* So I if asked if she had been noticing her depression more lately, and she said, *Yes, that's why I came to you; it's becoming really overwhelming.* And I said, *Well, tell me this: is the noticer depressed?* And she was stumped because, you see, the noticer can't be depressed. The noticer is the compassionate witness and we can go there and literally become the witness to our lives and our thoughts. That's the beauty of meditation. When you first are learning to meditate, your thoughts are all ego-based and anything that's ego-based thinks it's more important than anything else. So each one of your thoughts is saying, *Think me.* Then another one says, *No, think me.* And as you watch this, you become amused by it and you make a separation. Did you ever read *Siddhartha?* It's a wonderful story by Herman Hesse—the story of Buddha as a young man. Siddhartha Gautama Buddha. And he was fasting. He fasted for fifty days while he was going through his awakening period. And his friend said to him, *What good is fasting?* and Siddhartha had this wonderful line, he said, *I can laugh at hunger.* And he was really making a distinction between that which is watching and that which *is.* His body couldn't, but he could. Learning to laugh at hunger and fatigue and silliness and stress is really a dynamite place to get to in your life. That's why I call that "making the decision to become free," because that really is freedom.

How did you learn about generosity of heart?

When I was helping people who were addicts—I was one myself—I knew that if you're going to help someone overcome an addiction, whether it's drugs or alcohol or food or whatever, most of these people think they've never had any success in overcoming their addictions. So they get stuck in this failure mode of, *I can't do this,* and I would always say to them, *You've had a great deal of success in overcoming your addiction; let's find some.* With the crack addict, I'd say, *Let's find the feeling that you had one time when you realized that you had done too much and you'd just had it and you just put it down.* And they'll say, *Oh yeah,* because anybody that's been involved in that stuff has had experiences like that, *Oh, I went seven days.* So I'll say, *Seven days! Well, let's go through those seven days—that shows incredible strength!* That's one of those things that Maslow taught me, that you don't try to motivate people on the basis of trying to repair deficiencies; that's a really yucky way to try to get ahead of anything. You can't say, *I will like myself when I am no longer addicted. I will love myself when I am no longer fat.* Versus, *I love myself now and I can grow from this position.* So as a therapist, I always went to the success. Sometimes you have to really dig, but you can always find a success, and that's all that generosity of spirit is. It's just having the faith that there's always something positive in every human being.

The Kabbalah teaches that you have to generate a lot of energy to go from being a physical being to being a spiritual being. It takes a lot of energy. And in order to generate this energy, you have to first experience a fall. Every spiritual advance in your life is usually preceded by a fall of some kind. If you're a high jumper, you run up to the bar and you get as low as you can, and that generates the energy to propel you to a higher level. Well, that works with all things. So every fall of our life is really part of the process of spiritual advance. You look through the divorces and the fires and the bankruptcies and the accidents. In *All Quiet on the Western Front* it says, *There are no atheists in the foxhole.* When you get down to the point where you're really facing your demise, you find the sacred part of yourself real fast.

Some writers force themselves to write and then work what they've written into something; others wait for inspiration.

Interesting word, because when I write, I feel most inspired. I know it's what I'm here for—writing and speaking. The more I surrender, and allow that, it's like when they asked Picasso how he could paint the way he did, and he answered, *When I enter the studio to paint, I leave my body at the door.* The way the Muslims leave their shoes when they enter the mosque. That's kind of what I've learned to do with the last two or three books that I've written, particularly this one. No outline. Just sort of an idea of a question I wanted to answer which was how can I get the higher part of myself to triumph over this false ego that propels most of us in our lives. When I'm writing, I am completely and totally inspired, and when you're inspired in your life, everything seems to work. You feel better physically; money problems seem to disappear; your relationships seem to be better; you don't get annoyed by all the petty little things in your life. The word *inspired* comes from *in spirit*. When you're not in spirit, you are in ego. And when you are in ego, you have to try to prove yourself, you have to show how important you are, you're concerned about how many books you're going to sell, how much money you're going to make, whether it's going to be on the bestseller list, whether people are going to like it or not, what the reviews are going to say. That's all ego. When you're not concerned with that, when you're detached from the fruits of your labor, you can then be inspired; you can just let it flow. Whatever comes out is what comes out. I've written fourteen books, but I don't think of myself as a writer. I think of myself as a messenger. And when it's time to write, I know it. It's an overwhelming internal urge that I can't stop.

Where do you feel it?

I feel it in all parts of my being. I feel it in my stomach; I feel it in my mind; I feel, *I've just got to do this now.* I can't stop myself. How do you know when you're in love with someone? I think you can learn to live with just about anyone—if they took you and I and stuck us in a cell someplace and said, *All right, this is your companion for the rest of your life,* we could learn to love each other, even if you're annoying and I act stupid, we could learn—but I don't think that's really love. I think love is the person you can't live without. That person shows up in your life and you go through your relationships with that person and you break up and you say, *All right, I'm not calling,* and you change your phone number so they won't call you, and you're just really working on yourself, and all of a sudden you're walking down her street. It's the person you can't stop thinking about and you ask where that shows up in your body, well, hell it shows up everywhere— try to think of a place it doesn't show up. If you said to me, *You can never go kayaking again,* I'd say, *All right, I can handle that.* I enjoy kayaking, but now a friend of mine in Maui who is a kayaker, that's what he's about. If you say to me, *You can never* write *again,* I would probably find a way. And I think all of us have something like that in us. When it starts showing up and I sit down with my little typewriter and start letting it come out, I just can't tell you—it's orgasmic, it's so wonderful.

Do you see any conflict between the idea that things are as they should be, and, on the other hand, wanting to address societal problems.

No, I don't see any conflict at all, but then I don't have any problem when there is a conflict. One of the things I've learned, especially reading the *Gita,* and some of the other great thinkers, is that you're never going to be there until you can live with two conflicting points of view at the same time.

It's a paradox. We're a paradox ourselves so we shouldn't be surprised. You could just be apathetic about everything, saying that it's all in divine order so just screw it. One of my teachers said that hunger and starvation are part of the divine plan we don't understand. They are there. So judging it won't do any good. What also is there is your desire to end it. That's present at the same time and you have to go with that.

Now everything that you're against you have to fight, and everything that you fight weakens you. So whenever you fight something, you're the weaker for it. Everything that you're for, empowers you. So you have to learn to look at the things in the world that you would like to see corrected and ask yourself, *What am I for?* not, *What am I against?* They asked Mother Teresa, *Will you march against the war?* And she said, *No, but when you have a march for peace, I'll be there.* So if all of us who do not like war stopped being warriors, fighting, and shifted to *What I am for is peace, and that's where I'm going to put all my energy…* It's the same way with hunger. I've worked on the Hunger Project since 1977. I've committed a lot of time and resources and money. It's a project that was designed to end hunger on our planet by the end of the millennium, not based upon judging it as wrong, but on empowering people to do something about it. I am not against starvation; I am for feeding people. I am for teaching people to feed themselves. I am for people no longer using starvation as a political tool.

The reason the war on drugs is not working is because we make it a war. We declared a war on drugs at the beginning of the Reagan administration, in 1980, and since then, there are probably a thousand times more people on drugs than there were before. We have a million people in prison in this country for drug offences. A million people. Imagine that. We are the most addicted society in the world. We fill our jails and we want to build more jails. It's as if we could defeat AIDS by building more hospitals. So what we have to look at is what we are *for*.

I remember when Clinton became president, they commissioned a study to see what we could do about the drug problem, and they went to the judges, drug therapists, people who were involved right at the street level, and they said if we were to take all of the money that we are putting into punishment—something like ten percent is put into education and ninety percent is used for enforcement—if we were to just reverse those, we could end the drug problem in this country within five years. End it completely. They say we can't do that, that it's too politically unpopular, that we like to see the DEA and the guns and the big piles of cocaine, as though we're doing something, but we're not doing anything. Our children are on the streets getting addicted. So you have to look at what you're for. If you're for enlightened youth who know how to get high without having to use substances, then that's where you put your energy.

In your book, you say that telling someone to Just do your best *is a terribly demanding thing, even though people think it's not. It sounds like a kind sort of thing to say, but in fact it's horrible.*

It is. I never say that to my kids.

What do you say to them instead?

Just do. I remind myself when I go for a walk, I don't have to go for the best walk or the best bicycle ride I've ever been on. I'm a runner. I get up early every morning. I took the watch off myself about fifteen years ago because I found myself doing the very thing in running that I was trying to escape in the rest of my life. I don't have to do my best. I don't have to do it at all. The sacred self wants you to be at peace. The ego tells you, *You can do this faster. You're better than, you're stronger than, you're not getting old,* all of those things. The higher self says, *Just be peaceful.* And that's what you have to remind yourself with your children as well. There are some classes that you're going to take in school that you're going to want to do as well as you know how to do, the ones that really are intriguing to you, and there are other classes that you've just got to get through. I could never figure out why anybody ever took algebra. Or geometry. I remember them saying, *Someday you'll use this.* Well, I'm fifty-five now, still haven't used those. So when my kids say how dumb that is, I just say, *Of course, it's dumb. There's a lot of things that are dumb. So just get through it.* Or if they've got a teacher they don't like, then you don't judge that person, you just figure, *I gotta get through this.* That's what an intelligent person does, rather than fight it and get mad. I think the greatest lesson you can learn in relationships with everyone in your life—if you can learn this, you've mastered the secret of relating to human beings—when you have a choice, and you always do, to be right or to be kind, just pick kind. That's all it takes. Your ego says, *No, no, no, I am* right *here and she's wrong and I'm going to show her.* Your higher self says you don't have to do that. Men are really, really horrible at this, needing to be right all the time. Suppose you say, *We went shopping last week and bought a new toaster; it was $29.95; we got it on sale.* And I know, because I got the receipt in my pocket, that we paid $24.95. So that's five points, five dollars, for the ego. I can hardly wait for you to stop talking, even if it's in front of other people, to point out I got the proof right here. Or I can say, *Yeah, it was right around there.* And most people can't do that. They have to be right. They have to make the other person wrong.

Do you have a favorite food or meal?

I grew up in foster homes and an orphanage so I have sort of a foster home approach—I can eat anything. It's not what you eat that poisons your body; it's what you believe about what you eat. So the tofu eaters are in trouble. I think the survivors of the future are the ones who can eat plastic and drink industrial waste, because that seems to be what we're going to have left. I eat mostly vegetables and fish, but I love everything. I can't think of a thing in this world that I don't like to eat. I go out to restaurants with people who want to know, *What is it made of? Does it have this kind of oil in it? Where did it grow up? Is it organic?* And I think, *These people are so ego-involved.* They think their body is who they are and it's so important.

You talk about ego a lot, almost like it's a bad thing. It seems to me that ego is really just a defense mechanism that sometimes doesn't know when to stop. I'm wondering if we grew up feeling more secure, if our egos would work as more constructive agents for us. I just find it hard to believe that something that is so much a part of us is wholly a negative thing.

You have to remember there is no ego. You do an autopsy, you'll never find one. What it is is an idea. It's an idea that says, *I am separate from, and I am special, and I am important.* Your ego would have you believe that you're something that you're not. It would have you believe that your shadow is who you are. The shadow self or the false self. It's what keeps us rooted in the incarnate world that we are in, but it has us completely convinced that we have to do all of these things in order to be successful and healthy and happy. I don't want it to be perceived as bad. I don't use words like conquer or defeat when I talk about it. I talk in terms of taming it, just not allowing it to be the primary force in your life. And the way that you do it is what Vivacananda said. He said, *Go out and look at the blossoms on the trees in the springtime. Just as the blossom vanishes as the fruit grows, so too will the lower self vanish as the divine grows within you.* So you let the divine grow within you and then that part that propels you to prove yourself to be separate will subside.

Ellen Gilchrist

I remember this day as though it were yesterday.

Ellen Gilchrist was born in the Mississippi Delta in Issaquena County. Her first job, at fourteen years of age, was writing a column called "Chit and Chat about This and That" for a local Franklin, Kentucky, paper. Her first collection of short stories, *In the Land of Dreamy Dreams,* was published by the University of Arkansas Press in 1981 and reissued in hardcover and trade paperback by Little, Brown and Company in 1985. Little, Brown published Gilchrist's first novel, *The Annunciation,* in 1983, and her second collection of short stories in 1984, *Victory over Japan,* for which she received the American Book Award for Fiction. Her more recent books, also published by Little, Brown, have been *Drunk with Love, Falling through Space: The Journals of Ellen Gilchrist, The Anna Papers, Light Can Be Both Wave and Particle: A Book of Stories, I Cannot Get You Close Enough,* and her most recent novel, *Net of Jewels,* published in 1992. These two latest titles have both been best-sellers. She has received numerous awards for her poetry and fiction, including the Mississippi Institute of Arts and Letters Literature Award three times.

Gilchrist presently lives in Fayetteville, Arkansas.

ELLEN GILCHRIST
Desecration

*J*did not know they were going to paint swastikas on the church. I did not know they were even in the church. I did not know where they were taking me.

My name is Aurora Harris and I have been an extremely good and reliable person most of my life and in Gifted and Talented since they tested me in second grade. My father is the head of the English department at the university and my mother is a housewife and former painter. I am the oldest of two children. My little sister is not in Gifted and Talented because she has no self-esteem, which is not my fault, and doesn't test well. She is spoiled rotten, to tell the truth, and one reason I ended up on that altar is because my mother is so busy spoiling Annie she never has time for me. All she does is drive Annie around to art classes and acting classes and ballet classes and everything they can think of to develop her potential. Meanwhile, *I did not get elected cheerleader,* and if you think it's possible to go to Webster Junior High School and not be a cheerleader you have another think coming. I was conditioned to think being cheerleader was the main reason to go to junior high. Is it my fault I tipped over into the criminal element when I did not get elected? Not to mention I got fat. First I did not get elected and then I got fat and then I fell in with Charlie Pope and the next thing I knew I was lying on an altar in a nightgown.

Thank God for my dog, Queen Elizabeth. She may be little and she may be handicapped but she will bite, and everyone in Fort Smith knows it. She bit the mailman, and because of that we do not have our mail delivered to the house. She bit a woman who came by selling cosmetics and almost cost my father all his money in a lawsuit. She has snapped at half the people at the

junior high school when she follows me to school. I wish she would bite most of them. Not that the student body got to vote, as if we were in a democracy or something. No, the teachers vote, and it is based on who is sucking up to them the most, and I do not suck up to people no matter what.

It was four days after I did not get elected that I met Charlie for the first time. I had seen him in the halls, wearing his leather jacket and with his hair dyed blue and six earrings in each ear. You had to notice him, but that was when I was still trying to get the popular kids to like me, so I just nodded to him and passed him by. Now it was four days after my three best friends went off to their first cheerleading practice and all I'd been doing for those four days was moping around and walking home by myself about three blocks and hour. I even threw up one day. I swear I did. I just walked into the house and threw up several times. I could tell I was on my way to having an ulcer from only three months at Webster Junior High, but I didn't tell my parents. They are very nervous about me as it is. I didn't want to make them suffer or get them thinking about taking me back to the psychiatrist who gave me those drugs last year. So I kept my mouth shut and ate some crackers and peanut butter for supper and played with my dog. She is a mutt we saved from death at the pound and she loves me when all else fails.

Here's what happened next. It was Autumnfest, when all the stores downtown block off the streets and have carnival games and everyone is supposed to walk around admiring the maple trees and buying cotton candy and cookies from the AIDS task force and the Humane Society and the women's shelter. I'd been going every year for years. But this last time my three best friends were going with the other cheerleaders and I was left out. I wandered on down there on my bike. They were all still talking to me. They were trying to act like nothing was different. But the minute I saw them I thought, ride on by, don't even talk to them, and that's exactly what I did. I rode around behind the Bank of Fort Smith to where they had some game. Someone had come in from Fayetteville with this huge mattress made of Velcro and for twenty-five cents you could run at it and stick yourself to it. It was against the back of the brick bank building and there were these filthy looking jackets covered with Velcro that you wore so you'd stick when you hit the mattress.

Three or four boys I knew were forking over quarters as fast as they could get them out of their pockets. Charlie Pope was standing off to one side with his hands in his pockets looking contemptuous. As soon as he saw me watching him he got out a package of cigarettes and lit one and started smoking it. I have been taught that contempt for human frailty is a cardinal sin. That's my dad's strongest indictment. *Pride, Greed, Ignorance, Fear, Desire, the five daughters of Maya, King of Darkness,* that's what it says over my mother's kitchen stove. He moves the sign around and changes it. For a long time it said, underneath the five main cardinal sins, *Contempt for human frailty is self-hate.* What does he know about how it feels to not get elected cheerleader when you are the smartest girl in second, third, fourth, fifth, and sixth grades? Now they are going to make you a second-class citizen by a system you never agreed to be part of. I looked Charlie Pope in the eye. Obviously, he was running his own show. I guessed I could get used to the earrings. I walked over to his side of the parking lot and said, "Hello, how you doing?"

"You want to throw yourself at the Velcro?" he asked. "I'm paying."

"Sure. Why not? Have you done it?"

"Are you kidding? Here, have a turn." He fished a quarter out of his pocket and held it out to me. His hands were not that clean and I could see the end of the snake he had tattooed on his wrist curling down to meet the inside of his palm. At any other time this might have grossed me out, but not today.

"I have plenty of money," I said. I turned my back to him and walked over to the guy selling tickets and bought four of them and put on one of the jackets and hurled myself against the wall. At the last minute I jumped as high as I could and ended up stuck to the wall about five feet off the ground. The crowd roared its approval. I did it a couple of other times but never managed to get that high again. I gave the last ticket to a kid I knew and put my own jacket back on.

"You want to hang out?" Charlie asked. "Let's walk up to the square."

"Sure," I said and walked along beside him. Now that I was nearer I could tell he was pretty strong and tall for a boy in the ninth grade. He started to pique my imagination. I have an extremely active imagination. It has always been difficult to keep me from being bored if there isn't plenty for me to do. That is what the psychiatrist told my parents last year when they sent me to him to get over my trauma after one of my dad's students killed himself and we had to have the funeral.

"Did you read about that bear that got loose?" Charlie asked. "It's the same one who came to town last spring. They stapled a tag to his ear when they caught him last year. I think it sucks to staple things to animals' ears. He probably came back to get revenge."

"You should talk. With all those earrings in your ears. God, doesn't that hurt?"

"No. You ought to do it. You're a big enough girl to have your ears pierced. Why don't you do it?"

"Because my grandfather is a biologist. He would go crazy if I put holes in my ears. He is paying me two thousand dollars a year not to smoke until I grow up."

"What's that got to do with piercing your ears?"

We had arrived at the corner of the square and there were my parents, coming along the street in my direction. I told Charlie good-bye and walked on over to meet them. They are good people. Don't get me wrong. They understood that cheerleading failure had an effect on me. They just never could understand the breadth of what it meant. They went on to other things. They didn't have to go to Webster Junior High every single weekday of their lives and pass their three best friends in their white and green uniforms. It was intolerable. It has ruined my life. There is no fixing this.

Let's say that is no excuse. Well, it's at least a reason. I was in that church when the cops came and my name was in the papers and now I am going to have to go to Lausanne in Memphis which will cost all the money I could have had for college and even there the story will be known. I am a marked woman. There is nothing left to do but go on and try to get into medical school and go to Zaire and try to save some kids from dying of Ebola. I mean it. That's the only thing I think of now. I will finish high school and college. Work my way though medical school. Stay up all night being an intern and then go to some foreign country that needs me, and save lives. My life is finished in the USA. There is nothing left for me here.

I didn't get involved with Charlie right away after the Velcro incident. I was too busy having my life go from bad to worse. My grades got lower and lower. I sank so low that I even got a D in science, my favorite subject. I lost my will to live after the cheerleading contest. I really did. I used to have nightmares about it. I would be sitting there at my desk and Mr. Harmon would get up and read the list of girls who made it and my name was not there. That's it. The day my life ended.

I've been trying not to think like that. This friend of Dad's who's always been nice to me, this English teacher, gave me a copy of a new translation of Rilke and I read that for a while; then I just started reading Stephen King and Anne Rice and crap like that. At least I could talk to the other kids about Anne Rice. You think there's anyone at Webster Junior High who wants to talk about Rilke? There aren't any teachers that know Rilke. Well, I guess I shouldn't say that. So I started reading Anne Rice and you know I told you I had a very active imagination and I think it was because I sort of halfway started believing in vampires that I started talking to Charlie Pope. He looks like a vampire. I was running into him when I'd go downtown on my bike. He wasn't at Webster Junior High anymore. He'd been kicked out for skateboarding in the halls and was going to this school called Uptown where they put kids who are too wild for the regular schools. Except he never even goes to Uptown. His parents are divorced and neither of them wants him, so they gave him an apartment near the campus and he lives there with these other two guys and a couple of dogs their parents wanted to get rid of too.

It's really not that bad a place. I mean, Charlie keeps it clean. He's a nut about cleanliness. We have that in common. So I think it was the apartment being clean and him being nice to the dogs that made me think it was all right to go over there. In spite of the posters on the wall. There were some naked girls on motorcycles and some other gross stuff I don't want to talk about.

So first I went over there a few times. Then I started believing weird things he said. Then I said I'd go to the meeting. Then I let them blindfold me and got into the car and then I was at the church. I don't deserve to live for being dumb enough to even talk to Charlie. Much less think it made me somebody for him to act like he liked me.

Days and weeks and hours have passed since I learned my cruel, costly, bitter, crushing, stupid lesson. I am alone in my room writing this in longhand on a legal pad. I have given up on the computer. Charlie's other obsession besides cleanliness was his computer. He surfed it at night and slept all day. It was there he met other members of the cult he started. It was right there on the computer screen, where the CIA or the FBI could have read every word, that he got the idea to break into the Silas Mills Methodist Church and paint swastikas all over the walls and other stuff I don't want to write down and then put thirteen-year-old virgins on the altar and initiate them into the cult with sex.

I was not the first girl to be drugged and put on that altar. I was the third, and the main thing you must know about my dog, Queen Elizabeth, is that she bit him. They had brought her along in the car. I guess they were going to cut out her heart or something. Anyway, when they brought me into the church I started trying to get away. They'd given me some kind of pill Charlie stole from his mother's bathroom, but it quit working when I saw that mess on the walls. "Get me out of here," I said.

"Calm down," Charlie answered, and his stupid friend Lamont tried to get a half nelson on my arms, forgetting that my father wrestled in college and has taught me everything I need to know to protect myself. I elbowed him and when he reached for my neck, I kicked him in the stomach. About that time, Queen Elizabeth broke free and bit Charlie on the shin. Not some tiny little bite that will heal in a few days, but a real bite from the wildness that resides in even the most domesticated animal.

Then the cops broke in. They were coming in every door and they were not in the mood to think anything was funny. It would have been better for me if I had been tied up or handcuffed, but that's water under the bridge.

I am still a virgin you will be glad to hear. Not that it matters after my name was in the papers. Well, not my name because that's against the law, but enough so that everyone in Fort Smith knows it was me. Not to mention my parents told everyone they knew. I hate that in them. They think the unexamined life is not worth leading and that you must live so that you can admit everything that happens. That was okay back in the sixties when they were young but it doesn't work anymore. There are too many people now and most of them don't think it is a cardinal sin to sit in judgment or be contemptuous.

I have to wash the windows at the church every Saturday afternoon for the rest of my life. I owe them five hundred and sixty-two dollars for my part in the desecration of their paint job. I am paying it back out of my allowance and baby-sitting money until I go off in the fall to Lausanne or Saint Stephen's in Austin or maybe All Saints in Vicksburg, Mississippi.

Several times I have tried to make a list of the things that led up to me being on that altar. I have changed the order several times. I have left out a couple of events I do not think it's good to dwell upon. This is the best I can do and I am going to put this on the Internet as a warning to other young girls like me. Here it is.

1. Thinking I wanted to be a cheerleader and spend my afternoons jumping up and down and saying mindless, boring, repetitious cheers.

2. Being told by my grandmother how she was a cheerleader in Pine Bluff and was also the homecoming queen.

3. Being told by my mother that she was a cheerleader in Helena and how popular she was.

4. Ever reading or saying the word *popular,* which only means you are so dumb or stupid or easily influenced that you want a lot of people you don't know to like you and vote for you for anything.

5. Getting sucked into trying out for cheerleader.

6. Not getting elected cheerleader by the panel of teachers who included an English teacher who had it in for me because I corrected her in class one day. She said T.S. Eliot was an Englishman when anybody knows he was born in St. Louis, Missouri.

7. Losing interest in school and starting to make bad grades. Only how could I help it under the circumstances?

8. Continuing to go to Webster Junior High School after I didn't get elected. I should have made my dad put me in college. I should have taken the Graduate Record Exam. I bet I could have passed it. I am a lot smarter than many people who get into the University of Western Arkansas. Many people my father teaches can barely read English, much less Rilke.

Well, that is all water under the bridge. That is spilled milk. I am going to be shipped off to boarding school with other girls who didn't fit into the scheme of things. Well, I have to go now. I have to study biology for about three hours to make up for the two weeks I was running around with the cult and didn't crack a book. Wish me luck. Don't believe everything you hear about disturbed teenagers. Most of us are sadder than you know. Very, very sad. And I'll tell you something else whether you want to believe it or not. It's not our fault. I didn't invent cheerleading. I didn't dump it right down in the middle of junior high school to totally ruin the lives of everyone except the fourteen girls who make the squad. I'll tell you something else. It even ruins the lives of some of them. They peak too soon and are never that happy again.

> Yours truly,
> Aurora Augusta Harris, age 14

Jamie Weisman

Me at two years old, taken in the backyard of my house at Lindridge Drive. I have a twin brother, and it was actually difficult to find a picture of me by myself. We were inseparable until we went off to different colleges. He is now married and lives far away, but we are still very close, and we still speak the "dog talk" that we invented when we were too little to talk to and about our first dog, Fireball.

Jamie Weisman lives in Atlanta, Georgia, where she attends medical school.

JAMIE WEISMAN
Otto

I have been left alone in this small blue Victorian house, not far from the ocean. It is the house I normally share with my daughter, Lisa, and my husband, Bob. They left this morning on a father-daughter camping trip, and now I am completely alone. I should not say completely; it is not really true. My faithful black dog, Otto, is here with me. In fact, if Otto's presence is enough to consider me accompanied, then I have probably not been alone in twelve years. Even when I bathe, Otto sits waiting for me on the bath mat. When I get out of the tub, he follows me, licking the water off my heels. Being alone in a house with Otto is a feeling to which I am accustomed. There was a time when I did not enjoy it, when it made me feel abandoned and lost, but this aloneness is not like that. It is bracketed. I recognize where it began, and I know when it will end: one week from now on August tenth, when Lisa and Bob return.

The camping trip was Bob's idea. He works hard and has to travel a lot, and he worries that he is missing out on our daughter's childhood. If he could, he would switch places with me. He would teach high school and come home in time to pick up Lisa at the school bus. He is that kind of father. On Saturday mornings, he and Lisa make chocolate-chip pancakes and watch cartoons downstairs, whispering loudly, "Mommy's asleep!" Last Easter, we had planned a visit to Disney World. Two days before we were to leave, Bob was ordered on an emergency trip to Huntsville, Alabama. After much discussion, we decided that, as the tickets and reservations were nonrefundable, Lisa and I should go alone. Bob looked so desolate when he dropped us off at the airport. Later he told me he had never felt so empty as he did the one night he spent without us in the house. When he proposed the father-daughter camping trip, he reminded me of our mother-daughter trip to Disney World. I asked him if he was keeping score. He didn't answer. Then he said, "It's only fair." He was a math major. He believes in fair.

In any event, it did not matter to me what the score was. It has been well established that I am a poor and unenthusiastic camper, whereas my daughter is a regular Eagle Scout. I agreed to the idea right away. Bob had prepared a long list of reasons. My husband has the very human trait of thinking everyone feels the way he does about things. It would take tremendous persuading to convince Bob to spend a week alone, but I like my solitude, as long as it is finite. Even after I agreed, he continued to list his reasons. All I did was nod and say yes, yes, yes. At last I took his head in my hands and declared, "Sweetheart, go! Otto will keep me company while you're gone."

Yesterday, I helped them pack for the trip, and this morning I waved good-bye, feeling excited and hopeful and a good kind of sad, not anxious. After they left, I sat on the front porch with Otto and considered my situation. Here I am, a thirty-eight-year-old woman in the middle of a rainless summer, suddenly removed from the people who have defined me. My daughter, whose day usually provides structure for mine, is gone, and the house rings with her absence. My husband will not be walking in the door at six o'clock, hungry for dinner. During the school year, I may have papers to read or tests to grade. I teach French literature at an upperclass girls' prep school. Many of my students have spent more time in France than I have, and their French is impeccable, but their ability to understand the literature of the language is sorely lacking. I assign only the most basic texts: Flaubert, Stendhal, Balzac. They have no sympathy for Madame Bovary, and they do not understand her boredom, though to me they are all Emma Bovaries waiting to crack. I am older than they, and I have the wisdom and misery of knowing where they are going. But it is summer, and school is out. I have taught the same class for eight years, and there is nothing to prepare or anticipate. My day yawns before me, blank and a little bitter. I ask Otto what I should do. He does not reply. I ask him how I got to this point, and he does not answer that, either, though if anyone knows, it is he.

Otto was a gift, delivered on my twenty-sixth birthday by the only man I am absolutely certain I loved. He is all I have left of that man, besides a few pointless letters and some odd gifts, the value of which is no longer clear, even to me. Jeremy is not dead, at least not to the world, but he no longer exists in my life, and it is less painful for me to think of him as dead than to consider that he is alive somewhere, probably in love with another woman. After Jeremy and I separated, Otto was with me through long stretches of silence. For weeks, even months, at a time, I felt as if I were deep underwater, where the sun could not reach me, and I could not tell day from night. If I opened my mouth, it would fill with briny seawater, and I would drown, so I stayed silent, flailing my arms and afraid to speak. When I would surface from underwater and—to my surprise and almost against my will—find myself talking to an old friend or driving to a shopping mall, Otto was always there. Often he was the only reminder that the person who was no longer debilitated by regret was actually me. He was the only one who spanned the time from with Jeremy to without Jeremy.

Even after I told Bob that I thought the camping trip was a splendid idea, he worried that I would be lonely. Again and again, I assured him that I would be fine. In fact, I said, I would love some time to myself. I used to write poetry. I would like the time to try again. I would love to read some new books, especially in French, which requires a great deal of concentration on my part. I would like to take long walks with Otto and let some memories out for air. I don't often do that when Bob and Lisa are around. I am afraid of getting stuck in a memory far from them and finding myself unable to return. I intended to accomplish great things during this week alone, but the first day of my solitude has almost passed, and all I have done is wash two loads of laundry, polish my grandmother's silver, and read a few of my old poems—only enough to feel embarrassed. I confess to Otto that I am waiting for the day to end so that I can go to sleep.

On the second morning of my solitude, I take a long walk with Otto. There is no denying that he is getting older. He is twelve. That makes him eighty-four in dog years, Bob always explains to Lisa when she is frustrated that he doesn't chase sticks or balls. I drive Otto down to a park by the river and snap on his leash. I know we will get a lot of attention at the park. Children cannot resist Otto. When Lisa walks him, she stands proudly next to him and declares to the other kids, who may be intimidated by his size, "You can pet him. He doesn't bite." The children approach Otto cautiously; he sits, still as a statue, except for panting, smiling, and accepting their tentative touches. For some reason, there are no children at the park this morning. There are adults, jogging and riding bicycles. Some of them glance at Otto and smile, but we are disappointed not to see the kids.

I walk Otto for a while, but he is soon hot and out of breath. He tugs me toward the water. There is a steep slide down to the bank, but Otto plunges ahead, half-sliding. I have to hold on to a branch to lower myself. Otto splashes in the water. He slurps noisily, then lies down so the water rushes over his back. He could stay there all day, but after a while I call him out of the river. He rises heavily and lumbers over to me, nuzzling my legs with his wet nose. I turn to go up the embankment, holding on to a vine to steady myself. Otto is a mountain dog, and, despite his size, I am continually amazed at his agility. He will bolt up the incline as soon as I am out of the way. At the top, I turn to call him after me. He examines the slope, then charges at it; but he falters, and then he tumbles back down. In that second, I catch a glimpse of his surprised and frightened eyes.

He stays at the bottom a moment, so I crouch down and call, "Good boy, Otto. You can do it." He tries again, but he cannot make it, and now he begins to whimper. I am momentarily at a loss. I cannot lift him; he weighs one hundred twenty pounds. I decide to push him, but once I am back down the embankment, he has no desire to go up it. I point toward the trail, but he waits to follow my lead. That is his instinct. Finally, I have no choice but to scramble up the embankment and ask for help. Two joggers come by, and I apologize to them for interrupting their exercise. I explain the situation, and they peer over the edge to where Otto is sitting, soaking wet, his fur sparkling with sand. They discuss together the best way to get him up, and one of them goes down after Otto. He positions himself behind the dog, and I call, "Here, Otto. Good boy." Otto lifts a cautious paw. I call further encouragements in the baby voice I have always used with him. At last, he makes a move. The man below bucks him up, pushing from behind, and the other man lies on the ground, reaching for his paws. Otto yelps as he is pulled up, but they manage to get him. He is shaken by the encounter, and he darts over to me for reassurance. I give him a hug, and I thank the men for their help. The man who had pushed Otto shakes the sand off his hands, then notices how dirty his shirt has gotten. I apologize, but he just shrugs.

"Beautiful dog," the other man says. I thank him. They jog away, and I return to my car with Otto, who is limping slightly.

I still have photographs of Jeremy, and all his old love letters, which were really more like love notes. He said he had to save his creative juices for writing, and his notes were artless, flat, and straightforward, unless he was quoting someone. Nevertheless, I have saved them. I haven't looked at them in years, but I remember there is one that just reads: "Hannah, I need you. I need you. I need you. I need you. I need you."

Jeremy used to tell me that the true artist was condemned. The true artist would always sabotage his own joy. He said he was not sure if he was a true artist—he was weak for comfort and pleasure. Then he would pull me close and rock me in his arms and whisper that I felt good.

Four months after we met, Jeremy and I moved out of New York City. We found a small house by a lake in Connecticut, and we determined to stay there until Jeremy had finished his new play and I my dissertation. Two months after we moved up there, Jeremy presented Otto to me on the morning of my twenty-sixth birthday. I was overjoyed; I had told him that I wanted a puppy, but I did not believe he would actually get me one. After all, we both knew we would have to move back to the city one day, and it would be cruel, we thought, to bring a dog to New York. Otto was Jeremy's way of almost promising me we would never leave the house by the lake, of denying the inevitable future.

The little house by the lake was separate from the rest of the world. Like Dorothy's house in the tornado, it felt as if we had been ripped from our foundation and sent spinning into the air, miles high. A whole section of land and water had come with us, and we were a new moon, orbiting the earth, too small to be seen in telescopes. The house was sparsely furnished, and I loved the feeling of space, inside and out. Downstairs was all one open room, with the beams exposed and the walls stained a pale gray from smoke. There was a wood-burning stove in the center of the room, and we piled up logs next to it. The logs brought in the smell of trapped water and moss, and the inside of the house smelled very much like the outside. The stove gobbled up the logs, and we could never keep a fire going all night. Every morning, we came downstairs to a thin ribbon of smoke curling up from the stove and sliding toward the crack in the doorway where cold air came in and warm air went out.

From the back window, I could see through the leafless trees to the cove where the lake ended abruptly in rocks and woods. There was no beach, and in summer, when big boats churned invisibly out on the water, waves flew into the cove and smacked against the rocks. The water was black. All year, it was coated with a thin layer of brown and yellow leaves. After a storm, the leaves would be pushed aside for a while, just in the morning, and then the black water reflected the dizzyingly tall trees and the roof of our house and the low-hanging green vines as sharply as a mirror. In the reflection, the trees did not shoot straight up; they leaned toward each other, converging, and their branches met as if they were arms resting on each other's shoulders.

Jeremy and I used to sit on the rocks by the edge of the lake and describe what we saw to each other. Sometimes I said things that seemed to amaze him. "You should be the playwright, Hannah," he would say, "and I should just wash dishes."

"Don't be ridiculous," I would protest. "You're a great writer. You know it."

He would stare out over the dark water and murmur, "I wish I did." Then he would point out a beaver on the shore or a snapping turtle. Jeremy knew things about beavers and turtles, how long they lived, what they ate. Everything interested him. At night, while I read dry books of literary criticism, he read books on natural history and anthropology, apologizing when he interrupted my concentration to share some fascinating bit of information, like the fact that raccoons mate for life. We would laugh and marvel at these things. The world was gorgeous and strange to us.

The morning that I received Otto was bitter cold. I woke

before Jeremy and crept downstairs. The fire was flat-out dead, and I shivered as I crumpled newspaper and stacked logs. I was wearing Jeremy's old flannel bathrobe and sheepskin slippers, and I felt him all around me. Sometimes, when he was away, I would sleep with his bathrobe just to have the scent of him nearby.

After I started the fire, I made some coffee. It was my birthday, so I figured we should have a big breakfast. I started to make pancake batter. I glanced around, looking for my birthday present, and had been disappointed not to see anything. Jeremy had told me that he liked to give presents when he thought of a person, not when he felt he had to. I had been scared to ask him, even jokingly, what he was getting me. I did not want him to feel trapped.

I could not figure out how he got out of the house without me noticing, but I had just started to pour the first batch of blueberry pancakes when I heard a knock at the back door. I slip-slapped my way over to the door, where I saw Jeremy's face filling the glass pane. He was cold and hugging himself, but also laughing. His black hair was uncombed, curling down into his eyes, and the early morning winter sun filled his glasses with white light. I opened the door for him and followed his gaze down to his feet, where a tiny ball of black fur with a red ribbon around its neck was huddled.

I lifted the puppy and looked at Jeremy. His face was blank, suspended, waiting for my reaction.

"I can't believe it," I said. With the puppy between us, I leaned out into the cold and kissed him.

His hands were freezing, and I tugged him inside and reached for the puppy. Jeremy had to finish making the pancakes because I would not let go of the dog. He was so happy, seeing how much he'd pleased me, and he kept dipping his fingers into the batter and letting the puppy lick them clean.

It took a full week for us to decide on a name. I ran through the luminaries of French literature: Émile, Honoré, Zola, Hugo,

Jean-Paul, Albert, Gustave, Claude. I came very close to naming him Marcel—even called him Marcel for a whole day—but the name did not ring right. I kept asking Jeremy if he thought Marcel was a good name. He told me it was my decision. It was my puppy, but in a moment of weakness, Jeremy could not help reminding me that I was naming a dog, a four-legged creature that eats table scraps and worse. At last, I gave up on French literature and named him Otto because Jeremy has a thing for palindromes.

I try writing a poem, but I cannot think of one original word to say. I used to play a game, just for the fun of language, when I was by myself for a long time. I would choose a letter and force myself to think of all the words, good exotic words, beginning with that letter. This afternoon, however, the words that come to me are all bland as tuna casserole. In my poem, I want to describe a recent news event, the drowning of a set of boy and girl twins on a Maryland beach. When I try to write, however, I cannot get past the thought: sad, so sad. The reporters said the undertow sucked them away. When they were finally found, the children were holding hands. I try writing just that fact, but I have to go deeper than that. I want to write a poem, not a newsbrief.

Otto sits at my feet while I crumple up paper. He is still limping, and when I try to move one of his hind legs, he whimpers. When I get up to move to another room, he follows me with his eyes. I call him to come with me, and he struggles to rise. He is favoring his back leg, and he walks slowly, thumping forward, pleading with me for something.

Bob is a kind man; kindness emanates from his every pore, and strangers are always dumping their hearts out to him. He dreads plane trips for this reason. I advise him to snap on the headphones as soon as he sits down, but he says he can never block out the needy eyes of whoever is sitting beside him. As soon as he turns to them, something magic happens. A floodgate is released, and they cry or sniffle or sigh deeply and admit all their regrets and indecencies. He says he wishes he were a writer so he could at least make use of some of this sorrow, but he is the farthest thing from a writer. He is a computer programmer, and he says there is no way to express sorrow with numbers.

I admit the same thing happened to me when I met him. Perhaps it's his size. He is a broad man, not too tall, with a round belly, and shoulders thick and soft like loaves of bread. Everything about him has rounded edges: his brown eyes, surrounded by shadows; his short, gray-brown hair, far off his forehead, loose and downy. We were introduced at a party, and I cornered him for the whole night confessing that it had happened to me, that shameful horror: I had loved, passionately loved, a man who would not or could not love me. A cold man. A condemned man.

Jeremy expected me to read every new line he wrote immediately. Each evening, while he cooked dinner, I would sit with his pages on my lap. Sometimes he had only come up with one new line or tinkered with an already-existing scene. He wanted me to read the play from the beginning every time, but he made it clear that it was not my job to criticize. He expected that from his friends who were writers, directors, and producers. I was his lover, and that meant it was my job to love.

There is a picture of me holding a tiny fish, the product of an entire day's fishing on the lake. On the back, Jeremy wrote, "She sang beyond the genius of the sea." Jeremy loved poetry, painting, photographs of grim little girls, their faces smudged with dirt. He was drawn to heartbreak, and with him, I found I was not afraid to let my heart break. Not only was I not afraid, I enjoyed it. Many nights, we held each other and told all the sad stories of our lives. His father had left when he was three years old, disappeared except for infrequent checks with no return addresses that sometimes cleared and sometimes bounced. It was odd that his father, who was essentially a stranger to Jeremy, must have still considered him and his mother and brother as next-of-kin, because ten years before I met Jeremy, his mother received a phone call in the middle of the night telling her that her husband had died in a drunk-driving accident in Michigan. She declared that he was not her husband, and she was not responsible for anything he had done. The policeman told her there was nothing to be responsible for. He had died alone at three in the morning on a quiet country road. He had driven his car into a telephone pole and rocketed through the windshield. He was not wearing a seat belt. To Jeremy's astonishment, he and his brother were named beneficiaries of a small life-insurance policy. They received ten thousand dollars apiece, and that helped pay for college.

I could not match that story, but I told him how I had been pelted with banana peels on the school bus and how my first date turned out to have been a joke. The members of the football team had dared Joey Morgan to ask me out and kiss me. Joey took me to Pizza Hut, where I was met with a barrage of Instamatic cameras. Joey smacked his lips to my face, then pushed me away. After the pictures were taken, I was dismissed, told to find my own way home. I called my parents to come get me, but they were out, and I hunched, sobbing, behind a car, an orange Plymouth Volaré, waiting for all the other kids to leave until I could try my parents again. I was fat and pimple-faced in high school. I lost the weight in college, and my skin cleared up, but a girl never really gets over being an ugly teenager.

Jeremy was always beautiful. He did not deny it. As soon as he was old enough to want women, they were there for him. He told me he could not believe I was ever ugly because, he said, I had a luminous soul. I said most men don't care too much what your soul looks like. I care, he said, kissing my eyelids. I care, with his hands on my breasts.

The morning after our walk to the river, Otto is limping worse than ever. I can barely coax him to his feet, and when I do, he seals his eyes and walks blindly and three-legged. He is panting heavily, and when he lies back down, he grunts. I smell something funny in the kitchen, and I see that he has thrown up. After I clean up the mess, I call the vet's office, and they tell me to bring him right in. They all know and adore Otto. They call him the gentle giant.

It is a struggle to get Otto into the car. I entice him with bits of cheddar cheese, and he hunkers along after me, but when it comes time to jump into the back seat, he lies down, puts his head on his paws, and gazes up at me hopelessly. I try to pull him by his collar, but he is not budging. I hold a piece of cheese in front of his nose, then put it down on the seat. He watches it dispassionately. Finally, I take his front paws and try to drag him into the car. I am afraid I will pull his legs out of their sockets or break something. Otto is not helping me, and his legs seem to stretch like rubber, so that, though I pull and pull, his body remains firmly implanted in the ground. "Otto, come on," I plead. At last he lifts himself up, and I pull as he jumps, and he lands on me in the back seat. I laugh and bury my face in his fur. Otto smells of dirt and salt and leaves. His fur is the softest thing I know. I love this dog.

At the veterinarian's, Otto and I wait in an examining room. The air is pink with the smell of antiseptic. The doctor's instruments are bobbing in a tray of blue soapy water like combs at the barber shop. They are shiny and silver. Otto is resting at my feet. When Dr. Pfister walks in, Otto half wags his tail, but he does not get up and demand his usual caresses from her.

"I hear you're limping," Dr. Pfister says to me and to Otto.

"We went on a walk yesterday, and he got stuck by the river. I had to get someone to help me push him up the embankment, and I think he must have hurt something when he got pushed. He's been limping ever since." I stroke Otto's head. He closes his eyes.

"You look a little tired, Otto," Dr. Pfister says. She squats in front of him and touches him under the chin. "Pretty bad case of dog breath," she observes flatly.

"Which leg is it?" she asks without looking at me.

"The back one with the white paw."

Dr. Pfister sits next to Otto, touching him in just the right way so he shifts and lies on his side. She runs her hand down his leg, and when she reaches a certain spot, he nudges her hand away with his nose. She tries to touch again, but he is protecting the spot. She has to hold his face with one hand while she presses again. He yelps.

"You don't like that," Dr. Pfister says. She presses harder, and he howls. "You really don't like that," she repeats.

Dr. Pfister looks up at me. She's a delicate woman with short blond hair and wide cheekbones, very pretty, the kind of woman Jeremy would have liked. He was attracted to intelligence, beauty, and kindness, not necessarily in that order.

"I think I should do some X rays," she says. "The tender spot is not in a joint."

"What does that mean?" I ask.

Dr. Pfister touches Otto's head. "It worries me," she says. "It could be cancer."

Since Otto has to be sedated for the X rays, they cannot do them right away. He has to have an empty stomach. Dr. Pfister tells me I can bring him back tomorrow or he can stay in the office overnight. I want to take him home with me, but getting in and out of the car was pretty traumatic. I don't think I should put him through it again. On the other hand, I dread going home to an empty house. I think for a moment. "You'd better keep him overnight," I say. I don't want Dr. Pfister to think I am a bad parent, so I add, "He has a hard time getting in and out of the car." Dr. Pfister nods. An orderly leads Otto away on a blue-and-white nylon leash. He is limping very badly.

"We'll do the X rays first thing tomorrow morning," Dr. Pfister tells me. "But the sedative won't wear off until late afternoon. You should come get him around four." I must look stricken, because she lays her hand on my arm and adds, "Try not to worry. It could just be a bad bruise. Even if it is cancer, there are things we can do."

"Like what?" I ask. I picture Otto receiving chemotherapy. All his hair would fall out, and he would be a bald dog.

"We can take off the leg," she says, matter-of-factly.

Women must be careful of doing too much for their men. With Jeremy, I got into a pattern of cooking and cleaning, even knitting and sewing. I was a regular Betsy Ross. He loved me best when I was doing things for him, and after a lunch of shrimp salad and blueberry pie, he forsook his writing and the stacks of other plays he was supposed to be reading and carried me upstairs to make love. Shrimp and blueberries were his favorite.

The first time Jeremy left me alone in the house, it was February. We were in the midst of one of the worst winters on record, and the snow fell faster than we could shovel it. After the first storm, in December, Jeremy had engaged a local man, Warren Bartlett, to plow our driveway. Warren charged us twenty dollars a plow, but he also jump-started our car, helped us put up our storm windows, and, in the spring, loaned us a lawn mower. He and Jeremy had a funny friendship. When Warren came over, Jeremy would leave his writing and tromp through the snow with him, down to the lake to inspect the docks or up the driveway to work on the car. I liked to watch them through the window. Jeremy was a full foot taller than Warren, but he hunched over when they walked together. When they returned from the lake, shaking snow from their boots, Jeremy would offer Warren coffee, and the three of us would stand near the stove, sipping the hot coffee and not speaking, except occasionally when Warren would offer some piece of advice: Buy your wood from Ben Carter, or Remember to let your faucets drip. Something like that. Jeremy took everything Warren said very seriously. He respected Warren.

Winter was difficult. Jeremy and I were on top of each other all day. I could not take my customary morning walks, and though I was as quiet as I could be so as not to disturb him while he wrote, he still claimed that I distracted him. He worked in the small and forbidden room upstairs that he had designated his office, and I stayed downstairs, reading books that might be relevant to my dissertation and dozing in front of the fire or, secretly, trying to write a poem. I kept Otto on the couch beside me, and his puppy breath warmed a spot on my stomach.

In retrospect, I realize now that Jeremy may have made up the urgent need to go into the city. We probably needed some time apart, but if that was the case, he should have asked me to go away for a few days. It had been his idea to move out to the country. I was an urban creature, ill-equipped for the wilds.

The car fishtailed on the icy roads as we drove to the train station. I held the puppy on my lap, and I worried that I would have a terrible accident driving home and no one would even know I was missing. Jeremy promised he would call when he got to the city and make sure I was all right. If there was no answer at the house, he would call Warren Bartlett.

The snow around the station was all ashy and brown with dirt. It had been plowed back into ten-foot-high drifts, each marked by a layer of mud, like sedimented rock. A channel had been dug into the drifts. To get to the platform, you had to walk through a narrow opening, surrounded on either side by walls of ice. Jeremy said he felt like the Minotaur in the maze. He walked a few paces ahead of me, hurrying because he was late. I was surprised when he stopped, suddenly, and kissed me. His hands, big as bear paws in their black gloves, held my face. "It's too wonderful in here not to kiss," he said. He glanced down to where Otto was sitting at my feet. He mused, "I wonder if he would find his way out if we left him here."

From inside the ice walls, we heard the moaning of the train as it arrived. Jeremy broke into a run, taking the stairs two at a time. I followed behind him, urging Otto along. We arrived at the top of the stairs just in time to see Jeremy jumping into one of the cars. The doors slid closed in uneven jerks. Someone called a good-bye, and I thought it was Jeremy. I looked for him. The windows on the train were salted and streaked, and I could not see inside. A little way down, a window opened, and a man reached a hand out into the cold air to wave to his wife and child. A few other windows opened suddenly, like holes sprouting in the side of the train, but none of them revealed Jeremy. Then the whistle blew. The train lurched backward, then forward, and pulled away. I stood on the platform and watched the pale yellowed eyes of the back lights fade into the gray mist of a winter afternoon, already almost nighttime. Otto nuzzled my legs. I picked him up—he was almost too big to carry—and we made our way back through the maze to the car.

Jeremy forgot to call.

That night, we had a winter storm. Otto and I huddled in the bed, and, outside, the wind rattled the doors and the trees bowed and swept melodramatically. Occasionally, leaves slapped against the window like desperate faces trying to get inside. I pulled Otto closer. I kept the light on by my bed, and tried to read a book: *Anna Karenina*. But I could not concentrate. The storm did not disturb Otto. He slept next to me, his rib cage rising and falling, steady and even. I pressed my face into his fur, and it felt good to touch something alive. Winter lightning exploded low over the edges of the lake; it was different from summer lightning, diffuse and smoky. There wasn't any thunder, but suddenly, my light disappeared. I tried to turn it back on; nothing. Then I groped my way over to the door and tried the overhead light. It was also out. I picked up the telephone, and it was silent. That was a long, terrifying night. I held Otto close to me by his collar. Every sound I heard was magnified a thousand times. The shifting of logs in the stove was an avalanche, and the knock of branches against the house was the pounding of giants.

When the sun rose the next morning, winking and jeweled over the frothy new snow, I knew I'd been foolish to have been so scared. Jeremy called that afternoon. I had told myself that when he called I should say that everything was fine and not admit that the storm had frightened me, but when I heard his voice, deep and hesitant, I buckled. "I heard you had a bad storm," he said. "Are you all right?"

"The phone lines and the power lines went down," I said. "I was scared to death."

I heard him sigh, and then his voice came out differently, as if he had handed the phone off to someone else. "Mouse," he said—that was one of his nicknames for me—"you know you are safer there than just about anywhere else in the world. Why won't you believe that?"

Bob calls that evening. He is at a pay phone outside the Quik Mart, and I can hear the crickets and frogs clapping in the background. I picture him there, leaning against the blue-and-white phone booth, light from a street lamp showered on his pumpkin head. He and Lisa have walked to town from the campsite to satisfy her craving for chocolate milk. They are having a wonderful time, he tells me. They went fishing, and Lisa caught a rainbow trout, which they fried up and ate for dinner. Lisa is sipping down her chocolate milk. Between gulps, she says she will talk to me when she is finished. Bob asks me if I am lonely. I tell him I am fine. Then I cannot stop myself. I blurt out that Otto is sick. I have always wanted to be the kind of woman who keeps secrets, who has a mysterious past, aloof and impenetrable, but I am an open book, more anxious to share my failures than my triumphs. "What's the matter with him?" Bob asks me.

"He's limping," I say.

"I'm sure he'll be fine," Bob tells me. "Maybe he has arthritis. He is pretty old, Hannah."

Lisa takes the phone. "I know how to recognize poison ivy," she informs me. "There's lots of it near the campsite. Daddy says I can only walk on the trails."

"Be careful," I tell her. "If you get poison ivy, the itch will drive you bananas."

"Daddy warned me," she says gravely. She sparks. "I caught a fish. Daddy says it's the biggest one he's ever seen."

I tell her that is wonderful. She is a regular Indian girl. We will have to change her name to Pocahontas.

She laughs and says, "No, don't change my name." Then out of nowhere she adds, "I like camping better than Disney World. It's healthier."

"You do?" I say.

There aren't many things that annoy me about Bob. For the most part, he is loving and patient and funny, but once in a while, I do see these streaks of competition. I refuse to be engaged. "I'm glad you like it," I tell Lisa. "It is very healthy."

Finally, I tell Lisa that I love her and miss her and I'm counting the seconds until she comes back.

"How many seconds have you counted so far?" she asks.

"A million and two."

She hands the phone back to Bob and I tell him the same thing.

At some point, it became apparent that Jeremy was cheating on me. He had emergency meetings in New York City. When he was in Connecticut, the phone rang late at night. He would hurry to answer it and declare loudly: Wrong number! If I answered, there was the immediate click of someone hanging up. He got letters with his name neatly written in blue ink and no return address. It was apparent, but not undeniable, and

Jeremy returned from his trips to New York with gifts for me. An antique paperweight, its glass yellowed and turning opaque like a cataract; preserved inside: a pink rose dated 1918. A book of Elizabeth Bishop's poems, which he would read to me as we lay near each other by the wood-burning stove. He ran his fingers through my hair, which was long, almost down to my waist, and whispered, "Love, Carlos, tellurian, spent the night with you, and now your insides are raising an ineffable racket." After he discovered that poem, he nicknamed me Carlos for a week. Once he returned with a pair of ruby slippers for me. After we made love, he crawled to the end of the bed and put the slippers on my feet. He tapped my heels together three times and told me to say: There's no place like home.

Now I look back, of course, and I know they were all guilt gifts. Oh, special, perfect, proof of how deeply he understood me, how he could anticipate my desires, but dripping with guilt, and though I have them all still, in the box with his notes and letters, they have soured and lost their charm.

I have waited patiently all day to pick up my dog. My friend
Ellen meets me for lunch, and she observes that I am lonely. She
lifts one eyebrow, which is what she does when she thinks she
is being wise. She informs me that I need Bob and Lisa more than
I think I do. Ellen is unmarried and proud of her independence.
She is leaving for Guatemala in a week to buy dresses for a
boutique in New York City. After that, she goes to India in
search of scarves and tablecloths. I don't tell her about Otto. She
thinks it is ridiculous that I am so attached to a dog. She says Otto
is only a metaphor for what I truly want, that I use him as an
excuse for making the kinds of decisions that, on the surface, I
feel are weak or unjustified but deep down are what I really
desire. Maybe she is right. But she has never seen Otto swim, his
head straining to stay above water, his paws thrashing, as he
pursues me in the lake. He hates to swim, but more than that,
he hates to be far from me. I know it is absurd, maybe even
pathetic, but I am touched by his devotion.

At four o'clock I call the vet, and they tell me the X rays are
done. Otto is groggy but awake, and I can come get him. When
I arrive, the reception area is crowded with dogs and cats. A black
Labrador retriever is staring up at a frightened gray kitten,
wagging his tail with a priceless expression on his face of
mischief, malice, and lust. The woman holding the kitten is
oblivious to the drama. She is struggling to balance the ball of fur
and extract her checkbook from her purse. The kitten's eyes are
locked with the dog's. The stale, salty smell of fur mixes with the
piney antiseptic scent of floor cleaner. The tiled floors are freshly
polished, and animals slip and slide on them in their excitement
to be reunited with their owners and then to leave this frightening place. I wait my turn and tell the receptionist I've come for
Otto. She smiles, and two round apples appear where her cheeks
used to be. "We love Otto," she tells me. "What a wonderful

dog." She looks down and says, "Oh. Dr. Pfister wants to talk to you." Just then, Dr. Pfister steps behind the desk.

"Hello, Hannah," she says. She does not smile, and I feel my heart sinking. My stomach starts to churn like it used to before getting a grade on a test or a paper. "Come on back," she says.

She leads me to one of the examining rooms. Otto is not there, and it feels strange not to have an animal present. She gestures for me to sit in the only chair in the room, and she braces her arms behind her, against the white Formica examining table. "We did the X rays," she begins. The room is lit with a single tube of fluorescent light. I can hear it buzzing. Behind Dr. Pfister is a poster of a little boy hugging a beagle. It reminds me to have my dog checked for heartworms. In pink letters, it shouts, "Love your pet! See your vet!"

Dr. Pfister sighs. "Unfortunately, Otto does have cancer. It's in both rear legs, all the way up the femurs. I could amputate both legs, but the cancer is spreading rapidly. That probably would not extend his life significantly, and I think it would make him very unhappy. He's always been such an active, happy dog." She stops speaking and rolls her lips together. I stare at her dumbly. A horrible blankness is on me, and I feel amnesiac. I have forgotten who I am. I am scared to test myself. If I try, I don't think I will remember my own name, my husband's name, my daughter's name. Then that feeling dissolves, and my shoulders fall.

"Is he going to die?" I ask.

"Yes," Dr. Pfister says. "Bone cancer is very serious and very painful for humans and dogs alike. At the stage Otto is in, it's irreversible. At some point, you'll probably decide to put him down before the cancer kills him. I don't think you want him to suffer."

"Is he in pain now?"

Dr. Pfister gives a lopsided nod. "He is," she says quietly. She looks to the corner of the room as if the words she needs can be found there. "Not excruciating, but significant."

"What would you do if he were your dog?" I ask.

"I can't make that decision for you," she says. She is wearing copper-colored lipstick.

"I don't want you to make the decision. I just want your opinion."

"I would think about putting him to sleep very soon," she says.

Jeremy finished his play, and a reading was scheduled at a downtown theater. I expected him to ask me to read a character named Amy whom he said was inspired by me. While he was writing the play, he would often tumble downstairs and beg me to speak lines he had written for that character. I would repeat sentences over and over while he sat across the table, his hands folded under his chin, his eyes narrowed in concentration. Finally, he would either shake his head and mutter "Forget it," or he would spring from his seat and declare, "I think I've found something there." He would plant a kiss on the top of my head and grab the pages from my hand, shake them in the air, and proclaim, "Yes! Yes!" I remember one line that I loved but he rejected. Amy is talking to her brother, who is bitter because his child is severely retarded. "We're all beasts," she says. "Lost, directionless. Stomping clumsily over an indifferent planet, and what passes for knowledge among us is as senseless as sand, and what passes for love … [she gropes for the words] we could die from." I must have said that line two hundred times. It was snowing outside, and through the glass behind Jeremy's head, I saw the wind blowing the sky away. The snowflakes, as they passed the storm light, glowed greenish-yellow. "What passes for knowledge is as senseless as sand, and what passes for love we could die from." I told Jeremy I thought that was beautiful, but I think he decided that Amy was not that wise. Or maybe he did not like the way I said the lines. In any event, he cut it out, and for the reading, he asked a young television actress to read the part. He told me he needed me in the audience. Readers, he said, were easy to come by, good critics much more rare. I said I thought I was not supposed to criticize. I smiled and reminded him what he had said about being his lover, that I was supposed to love. He said, "You're not all that good at loving, Hannah. I think criticizing comes more naturally to you."

I was stunned. "What do you mean?" I asked.

"Just that," he said. He saw a friend of his, and shot across the room to talk to him. When I tried to talk to him about it later, he made excuses. "I was nervous about the reading, Hannah," he said. "Can't you let anything go?"

The reading was an enormous success, and a few weeks later, he got a call saying that the theater wanted to use his play in its upcoming season. He was thrilled. He rushed to New York. I wanted to go with him, but there was no one to take care of Otto, so I had to stay in Connecticut. That was August. In a month, the lease would be up on the house. We had not discussed what we were going to do after that. I had made almost no progress on my dissertation, and my advisor told me I had better move back to the city. But I worried about Otto. He would be miserable in New York. How could I take him there?

Otto's eyes are glazed when they lead him out to me. He is limping worse than the day before, and he walks in an odd, abbreviated gallop, trying to keep most of the pressure on his front paws. He lurches forward, two-footed, and the back of him follows like a lopsided caboose. Normally, he would bound over to me, rearing up like a little pony and licking my hands, but now I am not sure he even recognizes me. I caress his ears and coo his name, and he moves his head dumbly around the room, searching for me. His nose is dry and cracked, and I lick my finger and wet it. I have to ask the orderly to come to the car with me because I know Otto will not be able to get in. Outside, it is still as bright as midday. The sun sets late in the summer.

There are small white moths hovering over the field behind the office building. Otto used to chase butterflies, leaping high into the air, always missing, and sometimes landing awkwardly on his back. "Will he bite me?" the orderly asks.

"No," I promise. He grunts when he gathers Otto in his arms.

Otto is as limp as a sack of potatoes. The orderly dumps him into the back seat. Otto stays exactly as he lands. They have given him a painkiller, and there is a big bottle of nickel-sized white pills in my purse that I am to give as I think needed.

At home, I have to tug Otto out of the back seat by his collar. He tips over on the way out and lies on his side, apparently unable or unwilling to get up. At last I right him, and, with much coaxing, convince him to follow me to the house. The porch stairs present an insurmountable obstacle, and though I do not think I am strong enough, I am able to half carry, half drag him up them.

I figure that after the ordeal Otto deserves a treat, so I bring some raw hamburger out to him. He is not interested. The meat lies, twisted red worms, on the ground by his nose. When I am convinced he is not going to touch it, I scoop it up and toss it in the bushes. I am not hungry either. I sit down beside him and stroke his fur. There is no one to talk to. I have no way of getting in touch with Bob and Lisa. Ellen will not understand. Finally, I end up talking to Otto, speaking words he has heard before. "Otto," I say, "I am losing someone I love very much." I start to cry. "And I don't know how I can live without him."

Later that night, I sleep on the couch downstairs so Otto can be near me. He cannot make it up the stairs to my bedroom, to the room I share with Bob. My hand hangs over the side and rests on Otto's back. I wake at four in the morning. The porch light is on, and I can see the outlines of the furniture in the room and the trees and the bushes outside, all hunched over and gray-green like everything, inside and out, is underwater and covered with algae. I know I will not be able to go back to sleep. I blink in the darkness and long for someone to talk to, someone to understand that very soon the earth is going to be diminished, to understand that and mourn with me. I consider for a minute calling Jeremy. Last I heard he was living in Los Angeles, gone there to write for movies. He might be listed: How many Jeremy Hollanders could there be in Southern California? But what would I say to him? And what could he do? Some things you have to swallow whole.

When Jeremy decided to move to New York City, it was I who made the decision not to go with him. I think he was relieved, though he had told me that he intended to look for an apartment for both of us. He asked me where I was going to go, and I did not know the answer until I spoke it: "Home, to Baltimore for a while. I need to figure out what I really want to do." Jeremy did not try to change my mind. "What about Otto?" he asked. I said, "I'm going to take Otto with me."

About a year after I moved to Baltimore, Jeremy called me. He told me he had made an awful mistake. He still loved me. I was the only woman he could ever love. He told me he would walk through fire just to touch me again. I squeezed my eyes shut. I had not kissed another man since I'd left Jeremy, and I was beginning to think that I was doomed and that I would never be able to love anyone else. I wanted to believe that what he said was true, but faith is hard enough to come by without being asked to believe something that has been proven false. "Jeremy," I said, "I don't think we should talk anymore."

"If I can't talk to you," he said, "I'll be lost."

I hung up the phone and hugged Otto.

He sent me a letter. I threw it away, unopened. I remember staring at it in the white plastic trash can, on top of the coffee grounds. I thought my salvation rested on throwing away that letter, but in the end I could not do it. I fished it out, and I put it in the box where I kept his other letters. At least I refused to open it. I have never read it. I don't want him to have the last word.

Lisa and Bob are not due back for another four days. Otto is steadily declining. He does not move, except once when he stands up and pees on the floor. I clean it up while he leans wearily against the wall. Then he slides down on his side again. At first, I try not to give him the painkillers, but when they wear off, he begins to whimper, increasing to staccato yelps. Ten minutes after I put a pill down his throat, holding his jaws shut so he will swallow, he quiets and then sleeps again. He is now on a constant diet of painkillers. He will not eat his food. I cannot even tempt him with strawberry ice cream, usually his favorite treat. I pet him lightly. If I put pressure on the wrong spot, his whole body contracts. His eyes are red and oily, and the fur around them is moist. On my own, I make the decision to put him down.

For some reason, as soon as I make this decision, I go upstairs and retrieve the box of Jeremy's letters and presents from the bottom of my closet. It has been buried under out-of-date Shetland sweaters for years, and it smells like wool and moth-balls. I pry off the lid and look at the paperweight and the unopened letter and the red slippers one more time; then I take it downstairs and put it in the trash can. But that is not complete enough for me, so I lug the trash can outside and run the hose into it. The ink smears on the letters. I leave them there, waiting for the water to wash away all those words.

Dr. Pfister tells me that they can dispose of Otto's body, but I want to bury him in my backyard. I am present in the room when she gives him the injection. My face is close to his. His eyes gaze into mine, and I tell myself never to forget what they look like, for I know there is love in this world that is not harmful, and it is the love I have for this dog and that he has for me. Otto's eyes are big and black as eight balls, misty and covered with water. I have one hand on his front paw and one hand on his head. His fur is still so soft—it's such a waste. He is older—in dog years—than either of my parents, older than my grandfather was when he died. He sat on the shore while I swam naked in the lake, while I tried to draw from nature what I wasn't getting from people. He was with me when I saw an eagle. Dr. Pfister drops the needle into a plastic box. She whispers that she'll leave us alone. Otto's eyes sweep slowly shut. He breathes evenly. I can hear his breath slowing down. I cry. My hand is on his stomach. It is rising less now with each breath. I push my head close to his face. He smells like Otto: buttery and damp. Then he is gone, not breathing anymore.

An orderly carries him out to my car. He is zipped up in a pale-blue plastic bag.

It takes me all day to dig his grave. Finally, it is done, and I drag the bag over to the edge and roll it in. I am sobbing. I pour the dirt back on top. There is much more dirt now than when I was digging the hole, and the mound winds up being two feet high. A colossal hole. Otto would be proud. It is early evening, and a light wind rustles through the leaves like rain. It's one of those nights when the sky goes out the back door, and it's suddenly dark. It's quiet enough that I can almost hear the ocean, and I think of the boats on the water and the fish and the sharks and the dolphins swimming, all oblivious to my loss. I crouch down and touch the earth that is covering all that remains of my dog. I try to think of something to say, a final good-bye, but the only words that come to me are Jeremy's. *A true artist is condemned.* What does that mean to Otto? And then I realize what a stupid thing that was to say. For all of us, the road narrows to the same point, and either we are all condemned—or none of us; either Otto is gone—or he is not.

Eugenie Doyle

*It was 1957 and all the other kindergarten girls at P.S. 61
in New York Ciy wore dresses and ribbons for school-picture
day. I remember feeling both slightly embarrassed that I'd
forgotten to "dress up," and also very comfortable in my
sweatshirt and jeans.*

Eugenie Doyle was born in New York City and has lived in Vermont for
twenty-two years. In July, she graduated from the Vermont College MFA-in-
Writing program. Though the cows are gone, Doyle still grows berries and
vegetables on their farm, The Last Resort, with her husband, Sam Burr,
daughter, Nora, and twin sons, Silas and Caleb.

EUGENIE DOYLE
Red Flag

FIRST-PLACE WINNER
Short-Story Award
for New Writers

*M*onday morning and the beef truck just passed by. It never stops here anymore. Our cows are gone.

At our old farm, our first farm down on Route 14 in East Brookfield, the way you signaled the truck to stop was to put a red cloth on the mailbox or on a fence post by the road. Any scrap would do, just so it was big enough to catch Jim's eye, considering he drove early, before he'd had his second coffee, and it might be foggy in the valley. I always used an old T-shirt of Tony's, deep red, dotted with battery-acid burnholes so it easily looped the handle on the mailbox door.

Here, at this bigger place, you needed to phone in a request for the truck to stop. I'd dial early before the boys set out, but not too early. Chink and his sons were cattle dealers, not farmers. So I'd call about seven. Chink would answer, "Commission Sales." I'd say, "Lisa Mallory in Whiting, we got a calf to go." "Who?" he'd ask, and I'd say, "Tony Camp's wife," to help him out. I kept my own name when I got married; I know it's too much for some folks to handle but I liked to start out fresh on a Monday, stating the truth even if it might be a little tricky for someone like Chink. Hell, what can you expect from a guy who uses a nickname from a customer who thought his real name, "Wisnowski," sounded Chinese?

Then, sometime before noon, one of his boys would swing the long, rattling trailer up to our milkhouse door. He'd dash in and come out again through my nice, hosed-down milkroom with the marked bullcalf in his arms. He stuffed it into the small section of the trailer away from the big cows. Does it make you sad? A baby going to butchery just cause it's a boy? If you'd a' carried it out and got peed on right down your front where a bull's thing hits, you'd forgive Chink's boys a swear or two. I just wished they'd use the side barn door and not muck up my milkroom.

But let's talk about sad. Sometimes I had to call about a full-grown cow. Now if a cow dies, you don't call Commission Sales, you call a different number for the "down and dead" man, whose name I just now can't recall. It's on the yellow scrap of paper in the top desk drawer. If the cow isn't dead but can't get up and there's no hope, then you call that same number. You might think it's a strange business to be in, more or less collecting hides and dogfood. But let me tell you, it's a needed thing and this particular fellow, Taylor I think it might be, is helpful and good at his job.

One time, he called Tony late at night after picking up a dry cow we'd found dead in the pasture alongside Turkey Lane. Nice cow, Mina, three weeks from calving; the whole thing made us shake our heads. Then we hear from Taylor he'd found a bullet in the cow, through the shoulder; we'd never even seen the hole, but that's what killed her. Some fool kid, some mean s. o. b. hunter, we will never know, but it wasn't anything we could have prevented and that made it some easier to swallow the loss. Taylor said he'd keep the bullet a while in case our insurance man wanted to see it. Now he didn't owe us anything, but he gave us some peace of mind.

Back to cull cows: that's what they are if they can walk but they are sick and not full of antibiotics, or, say, they won't breed or are just plain low producing. Cull. And if you want to think sad, I'll tell you about Jobena.

She was seventeen years old, the grand old lady of our barn. Tall, strong back and legs. A perfect udder, high and tight when full, it milked out like a soft glove with firm, well-placed teats. She was a smart cow, never shit underneath herself, ate well, chewed constantly, knew her stall, and produced heifers, one after another, except for the year she had twins. One of those was male, so of course the other, the little girl, was a freemartin, sterile, and should have been shipped off, too. But our daughter, Emily, pleaded for them. We let her raise them a year for the freezer. Baby beef, the sweetest meat there is.

Are you vegetarian? Does this make you gag? I can't do anything about that. You might as well not listen. There's tender articles about soybeans for you. Go on.

I want to finish saying about my farm. The small, family dairy. Anyway, if you want us punished, I guess God is on your side, because we're all dying off.

But Jobena: when it came clear that in spite of expanding to this bigger farm, every milking meant emptying our wallets into the gutter, prices were that low and costs that high, we knew we had to have an auction; we all agreed we couldn't put Jobena in the ring.

She was my daughter's pet, really. Emily learned to milk on her. That cow tolerated the child sitting on her back while I milked the others. That's rare for a cow, which is not the same as a horse, although I hear most children in America confuse the two. Emily made dandelion chains for her cow, called her "Jobo." She brushed her back and tail.

That last year Jobena's feet got bad, and in spite of hoof-trimmer and vet care, she got so she didn't like to leave the barnyard to climb on the hilly pasture to graze. Emily took the scythe in her ten-year-old arms and sliced sweet grass for Jobo's meals. She sometimes sat and flicked flies from the big, brown eyes. She rubbed her udder with Bag Balm for sunburn that summer, for chapping as days grew colder.

Tony said, "Jeez, Emily, you can't treat every cow like a pet. No wonder we can't stay in business." But he did a funny thing himself with that cow. Before the sale, he found her a home, on another farm. He just gave her to the nicest folks we know still in the dairy business who had room for an old timer; that meant a farm an hour away. There, she had her last calf, a heifer of course, but came down with milk fever. Tony went to help treat her, but she died anyway. Our friends felt so bad they gave us her calf.

Now Tony had gone down in our family Taurus wagon and just put that calf in the back for the ride home. Over an hour away and that calf never pooped or peed. "Sure sign of a smart calf," said Emily. She named it Jewel. All Jobena's girls' names started with Js. Emily wanted to keep it and I said, "No way, one cow in a big barn is a foolish thing." But Tony said, "Why not? We can't stop being fools all at once."

So the auction's over and done and Emily and Tony do their daily calf chore for Jewel, ten minutes in the morning before school and work. Their chatter and the clink of a shovel in the big barn echo clear out to me by the kitchen window.

This is Monday morning. When I see the beef truck pass by I remember the morning I came home from the hospital after having Emily. It was winter; a shovel was stuck into a huge drift by the mailbox. Flying from the handle was a tiny pink undershirt. My husband, Tony, announcing our baby girl, a keeper of course, no bullcalf, but announcing it just the same.

SHORT-STORY AWARD FOR NEW WRITERS
1st- 2nd- and 3rd-Place Winners

●◆ *1st place* and $1200 to *Eugenie Doyle*, for "Red Flag"
Doyle's profile appears on page eighty-two and her story begins on page eighty-three.

●◆ *2nd place* and $500 to *Julie Showalter*, for "The Cancer Contest"
Julie Showalter grew up on a turkey farm in Missouri. She has worked as a clown and a grocery checker, earned a Ph.D. in literature from Ball State, taught at the University of Puerto Rico, and committed marketing research in the world's tallest building. In 1992, at the age of forty-seven, she started writing fiction.

Julie Showalter
Julie Showalter
"The Cancer Contest"
There's a moment, an exact moment, during the biopsy when you know it's bad. The surgeon, the same one who said, "Let's just watch this," and "This isn't anything," stops joking with the nurse and says, "When did you first notice this?"

●◆ *3rd place* and $300 to *Amy Novesky*, for "Here Where I Am"
Amy Novesky will complete her masters degree in creative writing this summer at the University of San Francisco, where she is working on a collection of short stories. Her fiction is influenced by her beginnings in poetry and by a love of imagery and of language. This is the first story Novesky has sent out into the world.

Amy Novesky
Amy Novesky
"Here Where I Am"
Below me, receding from me, in the thick rug of snow smoothed by the falling sun, are my footprints. They will remain untouched, however momentarily, here, until the next snow fills the deep gorge of my heel and the oval shadow of my toe.

We thank all entrants for sending in their work.

MARY MORRISSY
Award-winning Irish writer

Interview
by Annie Callan

Imagine downing a pint of full-bodied stout, and swiftly chasing it with a whisky. Imagine how the combination might seize at your throat. Mary Morrissy's writing has a similar effect on the reader's palate. Her language is lush and sensuous, Rubenesque, if you will; but it carries a sharp afterbite that can scald the tongue.

Mary Morrissy

Born in Dublin, Ireland, where she now works part time as a copy editor for **The Irish Times,** *Morrissy launched herself on the Irish writing scene with her short-fiction collection,* **A Lazy Eye,** *in 1993. Her stories are disturbing yet poetic moodscapes, peopled by characters who hover near some precipitous edge. A kleptomaniac, an obscene phone-caller, a woman who oozes a green discharge—her female protagonists' quirky views of the world at once provoke and tantalize. A review of* **A Lazy Eye** *in the* **London**

Independent *claims that Morrissy "is not a glib psychoanalyst, more a cool but gifted pathologist under whose microscope tiny slivers of unremarkable human tissue are shown to be teeming with microbial life and mysterious mutant energy."*

In Morrissy's fictional milieus, there are "eggshell dawns" and "louring skies." Rain "dreeps from the sills." The following sentences are vintage Morrissy: "Irene would remember only a swish of serge, the clack of beads, the stiff rebuke of a wimple." And she longed for "someone to pause, hand on flesh, to marvel at this breastbone, that hollowed-out nape, the wing of an eyebrow, to stroke the shattered line of a rib cage or the ghostly shadow of a haunch."

Morrissy says she came to fiction writing "by a fluke" when a tutor in a journalism correspondence-course recognized her talent. She went on to publish in **The Irish Press** *"Young Writers Page," but it wasn't until she was on vacation in Australia that she decided, at twenty-five, that writing would be her career. Little more than a decade later, like cream rising surely to the top, Mary Morrissy's remarkable facility with words has earned her a place among Ireland's most celebrated literary talents. She has won the prestigious Hennessy Award for Literature. And her first novel,* **Mother of Pearl,** *hardly a month on American book-shelves, received the Lannan Foundation's $50,000 Award for Literature. Her story collection is scheduled for a summer 1996 release in the United States.*

CALLAN: *Mary, you've already established yourself as a fine writer with your short fiction. In the United States, it's generally difficult for a new writer to publish a collection of short stories first. Publishers are more likely to gamble on a novel. Yet you've developed your reputation with* A Lazy Eye. *Is there a different attitude toward short fiction in Ireland?*
MORRISSY: Yes. It's interesting because the first agent I had said to me, "I'll never be able to sell a book of short fiction by an

unknown author. Write a novel." Then I got my present agent who was wonderful and she went out and sold all these stories one by one and made about ten pence per story! In a way, it disproves this theory that you can't be published first with short fiction. And quite a lot of Irish writers—Anne Enright and Joe O'Conner—their first books were collections of stories. There's this myth that the Irish love short stories—and maybe the Irish market is more into short fiction because of the particular tradition of short stories there. But I think it's actually a myth— the difficulty is getting published, no matter what it is. That said, Scribners [in America] bought *A Lazy Eye* but said, "If you're writing a novel, we'd prefer to bring that out first," and they're going to publish *A Lazy Eye* next July, a year after the novel, so obviously they felt that for the American market, a novel would be easier to sell first off.

Although there are a lot of people who love to read short fiction, it seems that unless you're a known quantity ...

Yes. I can't understand why the short story isn't more popular. It's the perfect commuter read. It's perfect for people with reduced concentration from watching too much telly. Often the best adaptations for the screen come from short stories rather than novels because they're so compact and easy to get across in film. And in the States there are such great short-fiction writers, it's extraordinary that it's not more popular.

I think it is a popular mode—the Best Short Stories, *for instance, sells well. It's just the new writer who has to have written a novel. Almost like you have to prove yourself.*

Exactly. I mean, I have great admiration—not only as a writer for Alice Munro, but also for her commitment to the short story—this lifelong thing that says you don't have to write a novel to be a writer. Sometimes it's like Little League and Big League—you're not into the Big League till you've produced a novel.

I'm not sure enjoy *is the word, but I was really taken with your collection of short fiction. When I read it, I turned each page with a mix of anticipation and dread. Your stories—the characters in them—have a disturbing undertone to them. Is this an effect you deliberately strive for?*

I think what most of the characters have in common is that they're pretty ordinary people but they're emotionally in *extremis,* and they have a skewed vision of the world. I didn't actually set out to write disturbing stories. I suppose I am a bit taken aback that people find them so disturbing, because I think they're verging on normal. Except in obvious stories like "Rosa," where they abandon the baby in the department store, which is an act of complete moral abandon. But generally speaking, I think the characters are the darker side that everybody has. What I've done in these stories is to indulge the darker side and explore that.

Yes. I felt that dark side to many of the characters. They reminded me quite a bit of Flannery O'Connor and Carson McCullers—the Southern grotesque style where characters are often "freaks" in some sense, or outsiders, loners. It struck me that a lot of your protagonists are looking on somehow. They are not the hero or heroine, not the popular person, but often the one who wants to be in that person's shoes.

I'm interested that you see O'Connor and McCullers in my work, because they were two writers I read as a teenager and who were hugely influential. I don't mean necessarily in my writing, but as a reader. O'Connor is such wonderful, wonderful reading.

But I think what my characters have in common is they long to be the center of attention and even long to be at the center of their own lives, which they somehow cannot manage. They haven't taken possession of their own lives and there is that feeling of remoteness from their own lives, let alone being the center of someone else's life. For many of them, it'd be impossible. When they try to be that, they fail. Like the girl in the story about petty theft at school, she is so longing to be this other girl that she is willing to take on her sins. It is that yearning to be at the center, and yet when she has a chance to be at the center, she can't move in and take center stage.

Also, there's a similar situation in A Lazy Eye *where the girl wants some grand dramatic act to happen to her and she finds ultimately that all she's due is "retribution for bleeding in public"—a depressing conclusion!*

Yes, literally bleeding.

Your main characters are all female. You address female issues—biological cycles, menstruation, etc., and you portray them with pimples and all. That impressed me. You weren't afraid to take on issues like venereal disease.

Yes, a friend of mine said I should call the collection *Bodily Functions*. Again, because these stories were written over eight to ten years and I didn't see them as a body together, I was amazed to discover this sort of "obsession"—the physical being a manifestation of something emotional—is very strong in all of them.

Another physical act you address frequently is procreation, which one would normally consider a creative act—and yet, in your work, it seems to be turned on its head and becomes a destructive force. There's an ongoing battle between the notion of women having, bearing children, and trying to either get rid of them or destroy them. In one story, you quote that chilling ballad about the woman who sticks a penknife in the baby's heart, and in another, a girl drives a diaper pin into a baby.

Well, perhaps, if I were a mother myself, I wouldn't write the stories like that. I suppose it fascinates me—the whole notion of motherhood, perhaps because I'm not a mother. And the presumptions that are made about mother love and *Mother of Pearl* is the same thing. It's about a woman who really wants a baby and a mother who has a baby and doesn't want it. Such frightening presumptions that all children are wanted. What happens if a child is not? And there are all those ambiguous feelings which most all of us go through. There are times when mothers must hate their children and wish they'd never been born and my work is an extreme version of that ambiguity. In the story of the teenage baby-sitter (jabbing a pin into the baby's hip), there was one moment when I was kind of horrified myself. I don't know where that came from. But a friend read it and said there's a kind of "Sleeping Beauty" myth in it. And the awakening of the girl sexually ... But the violence in that story—it does disturb me.

The one about abandoning the baby in the store disturbed me as well. I sent that one off to be published and it was returned with a rejection note that said, "No amount of fine writing can disguise the fact that this is a thoroughly nasty story." It was a male editor. I found that in many ways, that is society's answer: you don't want to think that women can have children and abandon them. It's a kind of refusal to face it. In the last decade, there have been several cases of mothers abandoning babies. There was the case of the teenage girl in County Longford who gave birth in front of the grotto and nobody knew she was pregnant and she and the baby died. People think that these sort of grotesqueries are only in my imagination, but they're actually happening out there. That story is not just one distorted writer's view of the world! The stories are disturbing, but they're also facing those very dark things, saying people think this way and do these things. Why do they do them, I suppose, is what these stories are about. An attempt to understand ...

The story "The Curse" reminded me of the British playwright Steven Berkoff. He takes on issues which disturb audiences. For example, a gang of skinheads takes a baby to a park and clobbers it and Berkoff says, like you, that these things happen. But people have a hard time with that. In newspapers, it's one thing. But in fiction ... Do you think readers want a palatable read?

I suppose they do. As you said at the outset, I don't think anyone could read *A Lazy Eye* and come out laughing. Sometimes we read to be entertained, sometimes to be disturbed. But I think there's a tendency to shy away from these things. Then there's that whole thing about being a female writer, and male editors seeing periods and V.D. and they go, "Oh my God. Not another one of these women writers going to shove periods down our throat!" So to speak! But the fact is that it's so essential to the experience of being a woman that to ignore it seems ridiculous.

On the subject of males ... The Irish reviewer and writer Lucille Redmond says that she finds very few sympathetic male characters in Irish fiction. A lot of yours are shadowy, sinister figures who are not necessarily developed but are hovering in the background, often ineffectual. Probably the most sympathetic is Mr. Skerrit in "The Curse." He's at least affable and kindly.

I don't intentionally create them that way, but it does strike me that they tend to be shadowy. Even Mr. Skerrit, who has a good heart, is basically ineffectual in the end. He can't stop the girl being humiliated even though he's understanding. In the novel, there are obviously more male characters, and I like to think they're better developed. But men don't come out very well in my fiction. It isn't a polemical thing with me. That just seems to be the way it is in the fiction itself. I mean, the one story in the book that's written from the male viewpoint—I'm not entirely convinced of it. I think it's quite hard to get inside the male. These stories, in a way, are an indication of that.

I am fascinated by your beginnings. You have this uncanny ability in a brushstroke to lure the reader in. Such as: "At forty-one, Grace Davey's biggest fear was that she would dry up," or, "Her teeth must have been rotting quietly for months, but she only discovered this the morning after Jimmy left," or, "She woke up in a pool of blood." Do you start with a sentence, or an idea?

Well, I'll often start with a sentence. Maybe it's all those years working as a hack that the importance of getting everything into the intro [contributed]. I mean, I don't actually sit down and think of a good hook to get people in. In fact, often the first sentence will be the central notion of the story. Like the story of

Bella on the train: she woke in a pool of blood. In a sense, every month this is what happens to women; yet you immediately think somebody has done her in, and it was an attempt to say, this happens to women every month and there is something quite disturbing and strange about it, even when you're a woman and it happens to you all the time. As I say, I don't consciously set out to get a real humdinger of a sentence, but several people have said my sentences get them hooked.

Another strength in your work is the meticulous attention to detail. It's incredible. In an era of minimalism and spare, laconic writing, you seem to go to great and successful lengths to create a vivid picture. There are eminently quotable passages. Do you spend a lot of time honing your words?

I do, yes. For most stories, I do three or four drafts. I always write longhand first and then I go to the computer. They're very worked. It's something I worry about sometimes, that they're overworked, that there's too much labor and contrivance in them. I've always just been fascinated by that notion of "the thingness of things." That we're surrounded by these things all the time but we don't actually look at them and see what they're like. It's like if you say a word and you repeat it often enough, it begins to sound very strange. I think the same thing happens if you look at something ordinary and concentrate on it; it becomes absurd and outlandish and unreal. And that's what I'm doing—looking at something and repeating looking at it.

Well, it really situates the reader. I feel like I inhabit these stories as I'm reading them. On the notion of situation: I know you're an Irish writer living in Dublin. But these stories don't seem to have a particular locus or locale. Even the names aren't particularly Irish. The places are not ones I'm familiar with. Do you just make the names up?

Yes. Even though I'm aware that there is a kind of Irishness about them and about the way the language is used, the obsession with guilt and the whole Catholic backdrop to it, I'm very wary about setting any of my stories anywhere. I mean, I had a real problem in the novel, because it is set in an unnamed city, though it is definitely 1950's Ireland. But I didn't want to get bogged down with, "Did this shop stand on the corner of this street in 1950?" or whatever. And to me, the sense of place is overworked in Irish fiction.

I actually have this difficulty with using real place names. First of all, it's a bit like a journalistic shorthand. If you say, this character was walking down Grafton Street, well, for most of your readers, you don't have to say anything more: they can picture the street in their heads. It's a kind of laziness.

But it can be good for tourism! Like Joyce: you can retrace every step of Leopold Bloom's journey through Dublin now.

That's true. And in many ways, the other reason I'm not specific about place is because of Joyce, because he made Dublin so much his own that almost anyone else using the same street names or locales seems fraudulent. It doesn't seem convincing.

Or unique anymore. Joyce has the monopoly on Dublin.

Exactly. I mean, the difficulty about making up names is that then they sound impossibly stage-Irishy. So I try to avoid it and, in fact, I go into terrible contortions to avoid naming anywhere. Also, because I think it is—or has been—an obsession with Irish writers—you know, the little thatched cottage—all this sort of stuff… And I think the urban experience doesn't have that sort of relationship with the land. You know, I just don't think it exists anymore, or else it's been done to death. And if the world doesn't know that we're terribly sentimental about and attached to our little pieces of bog, then it's too bad [laughs]. If they don't know now, they'll never know.

The other element that fascinated me was superstition. Some of your characters seem to make pacts with the universe, or even with the devil, for want of a better word. In your last story, the final sentence in the entire book reads, "There was a curse on her now." That's a really chilling ending—after a gripping read, to be left with that. I'm wondering if that placement was deliberate, whether you wanted this as your last word.

My last word [laughs]! I didn't consciously decide that that was going to be my last word, although I did decide it would be the last story in the collection, partly because it's longer and I arranged the stories so that the big confession story would be in the middle. In a way, all of them are confessional in mode and also they're confessional in the sense that they're all about guilt. I mean, these characters are guilty for things they have done or guilty for things they haven't, or not guilty where they should be! Like the two sisters who abandon the baby. There's no sense of guilt in that story.

Yes, that's where you would expect it.

Then you have the girl in the moment of downfall who confesses to something she's not guilty of, and you have the teenage baby-sitter who goes for a baby with a pin and the curse that's on her is that she's going to be guilty about that for the rest of her life. Everything after that is seen as retribution for that act of terrorism. That's partly Catholicism.

And a very Irish notion.

Yes, and also the idea that you can bargain your way out of it. Like the woman whose father is ill. She feels as guilty as if she had murdered the young man in the war, even though she hadn't. She had just said to God, "Please take him rather than my father." But it is a mixture of perhaps pagan superstition overlaid with Catholicism. Again, it's very hard to get away from Catholicism, but it's a bit like the bog. It has been overdone in Irish writing too. But the thing is that it's implicit in almost anyone who's been brought up as a Catholic. You may stop being a Catholic but...

It doesn't go away.

It doesn't stop there, no. So you probably find in *Mother of Pearl*—it being set in 1950's Ireland—that there's a lot of explicit Catholicism in it that's kind of inevitable.

In your novel, one of the characters conjures up an imaginary sister. And you have several sibling—sister—stories in your collection.

Yeah, sisterhood is a big issue. I don't know why that is. I mean, I have a sister and we're very close, but there's eight years between us, and that's always created a kind of tension. She's younger than I am, which comes out a lot in the fiction. It's kind of curious because I have two brothers, but most people who read my work say they would never guess. They say, "You would either think you were an only child or else you just had a sister." Of course, I think a lot of writers write as if they were only children because deep down, they wanted to be. It's funny—the male side of the family doesn't come out, you know, and partially that's because I had quite a female upbringing. My father died when I was young and my brothers were older, so there was a *before and after* in our family ... *Before,* we were the nuclear family, and then my father died and my brothers left home. Then there was my mother and my sister and me, and the influence of that is more powerful than the *before,* which was the standard nuclear family.

Eugene O'Neill said happy families are all the same. The unhappy ones are different in their unique ways, and so more interesting. Flannery O'Connor claimed you get all your material in the first twelve years of your life.

I think that's perfectly true, yes. Patrick White says that for the creative writer, everything important that happens to you happens before you were born so ...

It'll be interesting when I'm started on another novel and also writing stories. I think a debut collection of stories from a first-time writer inevitably concentrates on childhood. It's almost *de rigeur,* really. The stories I'm writing now are less concerned with childhood, although there's always at the center the nugget of something that has happened a long time ago. Writers are recycling their childhood all the time.

In different ways.

Or maybe, they never stop being children is another explanation!

Interview: MARY MORRISSY

And a scary one. There seems to be a new generation of young writers—a burgeoning industry, so many it's hard to keep up with. How is it to be a writer in Ireland today? Do you think it's easier there now?

Well, I think it's certainly more conducive than it has been. I don't know why there are so many of us. It's partly perhaps a new confidence about Ireland and the kind of contributions Ireland can make on the international stage. Some of it has to do perhaps with Mary Robinson [first woman president], and obviously now with the prospect of peace in Northern Ireland, and joining Europe [Ireland joined the European Community in 1973] was very important for breaking that almost parent-child link with Britain. In a way, Europe is a bigger family to look out toward. But I think even small things like the success of the rockband U2 account for it. There's a feeling that it is possible to live here and work here and be recognized elsewhere, which up to now hasn't been the case. The development of communication and television has helped, too.

It's a generational thing as well, in the sense that a lot of my contemporaries in the writing scene are the last generation to find work here before the big recession and the huge new waves of emigration. I look at my sister, say, who lives in Australia, and when she came out of college there was no way she was going to get a job here. It was just automatic that she would go, whereas when I came out of journalism school, there were sixteen of us in our class and we all got jobs. It's maybe the fruits of the boon of the late 1960s, 1970s that we're the product of.

I'm curious. I've heard it said that women used to wait longer to write than males, that first they would raise their families, have their children, and then, if they had a novel in them, they'd do it. But you're a relatively young writer and there are many female contemporaries of yours who are writing now and not waiting. Do you think it is a better place today for women writers?

Yes, I think it is, although I still think there is this imbalance between genders. I've often wanted to sit down and work it out scientifically. I think you'll find that male authors will always get published sooner, earlier than female authors, regardless of whether they're single, married, with or without children. I think it always takes longer for a woman to get to the point of confidence in herself, to start sending her work out into the world. I know that it took me years and years and years to actually get to that point. Even to show work to anybody was a major thing, and so full of shame. And I don't think that male writers have that gap between taking themselves seriously and being published, whereas women still do.

Has that anything to do with the educational system in Ireland? Or is it innate?

I think it's probably innate because there's still very much that image of the woman as the muse and inspiration, but not the person who goes out and creates. That's not something just in the male psyche. It's in the female psyche. In time, hopefully that will disappear, but it is still there.

It's interesting too in terms of numbers. If I had a balance sheet, I'd have a much longer list of new male Irish writers than female. But at least there *are* emerging women's voices, which is encouraging.

And there are many. It is a great time to be a writer here. There probably hasn't been a better time. There's a lot of development of the Irish publishing industry up to this; they're really getting their act together, and it's gratifying to see that.

And then there are tax incentives.

Exactly. Your earnings from creative work are not taxed which, as you know, Ireland being a hugely taxed country, is a great boon. It feels that there is that attitude toward writers. I mean, there's still plenty of room for improvement. You still can't sign on the dole and say, "I'm a writer," or, "I'm working at home." But you know what they say: in every pub in Ireland, there's someone with an unwritten book in them. I think the climate is better now.

Interview: Mary Morrissy

Although it seems a lot of the new generation of writers have English publishers—like yourself [Jonathan Cape].

Yes, that's unfortunate, but in the past, Irish publishers have been notoriously bad to their writers.

In what way?

Well, this is one example: I won't mention any names, but I sent the collection of stories that is *A Lazy Eye* to an Irish publisher during the 1980s. I heard absolutely nothing—no acknowledgment even of my glorious manuscript. After two years, I got a letter from the fiction editor saying, "I was going through the drawers of my desk and I discovered your manuscript." I thought, even if I had done this, I would not write and say that, "Scrabbling among the orange peels at the bottom of my desk, I found your dog-eared manuscript!" He said, "Unfortunately, I'm leaving this post, but I'll hand it on to my successor and they'll be in touch." I never heard a thing again. And I thought, this is why Irish authors have gone abroad—because it really is no way to run a business, which is what publishing is. It's very demeaning, that sort of thing. There's been a lot of bleating about the unpatriotic Irish writers going elsewhere, but until that kind of attitude is totally banished from Irish publishing... It's on its way; that sort of stuff has mostly gone by the board. But if that's happened to me, then it's happened to other people, I'm sure, and who can blame them for going elsewhere?

Did you go through an agent to Jonathan Cape?

I did, yes. She had spent quite a bit of time sending the stories off, and one of them was published in *London Magazine*. Jonathan Cape wrote to me as a result and said they'd be interested in seeing more. So after years of trying to flog them, a publisher actually came to me, which was kind of miraculous!

An excerpt from *Mother of Pearl*:
   ... By the time Stella and I got home from school, the curtains were drawn and a curious hush prevailed that forced

us to speak in whispers. My mother sat on the bottom step of the stairs. Even her hair seemed bereaved, falling in wisps around her ravaged face. It was the first time I realized the sheer ugliness of grief. The puffy eyelids, the mottled flush, the messiness of it.

Two men in gabardine coats came to coffin him. I remember still the ominous thumps that emanated from the parlour as if a tussle were in progress and Granda was putting up resistance. The last we saw of him was his casket like a giant shoe box being manhandled out of the house. I could not quite believe that he was gone. I fully expected that when all the fuss had died down he would be back again in his spot by the fire. It made me more firm in my conviction that people did just vanish inexplicably, that in a moment's carelessness they could simply be taken away. I was only grateful that once more I had managed to escape seizure.

Annie Callan is a native Dubliner who now writes and teaches in Oregon, where she lectures in contemporary Irish writing. Callan also serves as Consulting Editor of *Glimmer Train.* Her collection of poems, *The Back Door,* was published last fall.

Jane Rosenzweig

In the yard, at ten months. I don't think I knew where I was going.

Jane Rosenzweig grew up in Pittsburgh, Pennsylvania. She is a staff editor at the *Atlantic Monthly* and lives in Cambridge, Massachusetts. Her first short story was published in *The May Anthology of Oxford and Cambridge Short Stories 1993*.

Jane Rosenzweig
JANE ROSENZWEIG
The End of the Decade

My grandmother died in late October, and on the first Saturday in November my father flew to Miami Beach, packed up everything in her apartment—from the good china to Grandpa Jack's seventy-seven issues of *Reader's Digest*—rented a U-Haul, and drove all the way back to Pittsburgh without stopping. Then, with no help from anyone, he carried it into the house piece by piece, and began to transform our basement into an exact replica of her apartment.

By that time, Uncle Maury and Aunt Candace had flown to Grand Cayman for their winter vacation. "Is this what you meant when you promised Maury you would take care of everything?" my mother demanded. My mother was used to having control of a situation, and when she didn't, what was left of her German accent would turn honey-thick, a sign I had learned to equate with danger. "I hope you don't think we're going to keep all of this *here,*" she said. My father didn't answer. "You know we don't have the space for all that heavy furniture," she said. Still, my father was silent. My mother stood in the kitchen, her hands on her tiny hips, talking to his back as he disappeared down the basement stairs.

I was an only child of sixteen, and, as usual, watching.

It was the end of the decade then, just before the seventies ran out of steam. Our home was Pittsburgh, on the edge of a Jewish neighborhood where not everyone was Jewish, and the more money you had, the less you prayed. On the Jewish holidays, we ate. Our family was small—only my father's brother Maury, his wife and their two sons, and, until she died, my grandmother. My mother was an orphan, a child of the Holocaust, who had weathered the war in hiding on a farm near Amsterdam. Her family was killed by the Nazis, but that was as much as I knew. She didn't talk to me about those years; in my mind, her life came into focus only when she came to America. The Holocaust was a vague presence in the background of my childhood, a disturbing painting hung in the drawing room, something that would always be there when I got around to examining it. I knew I was named Ilse after her dead sister, but I couldn't remember how I knew this.

The little I understood about my mother's past came from what I overheard—like Aunt Candace saying to my grandmother, "Of course, she had no mother of her own, so how could we expect she would know how to raise a daughter...," when my mother let me get my ears pierced before my bat mitzvah. Or when I was ten, after her cousin Jacob, the one who had been in hiding with her, shot himself in New York City, my mother sat all night on the back porch with a bottle of scotch, staring at a small gold locket on the table in front of her. I knew the locket had belonged to her mother. The rest of what I knew was from Anne Frank.

We looked like a normal family, but I knew we weren't. At sixteen, I was constantly taking inventory of surfaces—dress, facial expressions, conversation. As long as the appearances were convincing, I could breathe, I could tell myself I was normal, my family was just like any other family. I didn't have words for what made us different. It was just something I knew all at once, the way you know a color even though you can't describe it, the way you look at the setting sun and you just know, *orange, yellow, red.*

Whatever feelings my mother carried with her from her past were buried beneath layers of social skill and grace. She entertained frequently, was well-known in the community, dressed with a flair that everyone noticed. She was always being invited to serve on the board of something. She charted my father's law career carefully, complementing his shyness with a carefully measured charm. At home, we went through the motions of what I imagined happened in other families. We ate dinner together every night, a meal my mother threw together in haste between projects. Occasionally my father told me about one of his cases, demonstrating a truck accident at the dinner table with two forks and a spoon. Most of the time he was quiet, and I was ashamed to notice that I could spend a whole meal without looking at him, my whole body turned toward my mother.

She was restless in a way that drew people to her. You could see it in the way her activities overlapped, in the undercooked meat she sometimes served us, in the speed at which she drove me home from school with the windows rolled down, my eyes tearing from the weight of the wind. Next to her, my father, with his projects and his silences, seemed always poised to disappear.

The semester my grandmother died, I was busy learning how to be popular. I was home only as long as I had to be in order to do a respectable amount of homework and to sleep. My social success was sudden, and I had no doubt that my status was fragile. I had worked hard to grow my hair, choose the right clothes. Everywhere, I searched for my reflection—in mirrors, the oven door, car windows—to confirm that I was still this other person, the Ilse everyone else saw.

I had two best friends that year, both skinny and blonde, and we were definitely in the middle of things. Everyone envied me because I had no curfew. My mother wasn't interested in those kinds of rules, and she was interested in my popularity. The same

week my grandmother died, I had sex for the first time, at
midnight in a car parked at Kennywood Park with Adam
Berkman. This was part of my plan; I was becoming someone
else, now Ilse who was not a virgin, now Ilse who easily did
things like what I had done. It was a curious kind of freedom,
this dependence on seeing myself always as someone else,
always through other people's eyes.

The night we got the phone call about my grandmother, I
didn't know how to feel; I had not even seen her in five months,
had never seen much of her. My mother stood in the doorway
of my room and told me. "Your grandmother has died," she
said, as if she were telling me to take my umbrella, that it might
rain. That night, huddled under my comforter, I burned incense
because I didn't know what people did. What I thought about
was how I would wear my grief if Adam Berkman called. How
I would tell him and then cut the conversation short. How he
would want to be close to me, but I would be cool and distant.
He didn't call.

When we buried my grandmother two days later I wore black
from head to toe, a shirt of soft silk and a long black skirt. I
admired myself in the mirror. I could believe from looking at
myself that I was someone in mourning. "Don't you think that's
a bit sophisticated?" my mother asked.

"We're going to a funeral."

"It's the middle of the afternoon," she said, and then she
shrugged. She was wearing chocolate brown, a suit of soft wool.

Sometimes I thought I hated her.

She didn't say anything about what my father was doing in the
basement, not at first, not after she let him know how she felt that
first day as he emptied his childhood into the basement stairwell.
Nights when he worked down there she stayed in their bedroom, riding the exercycle or talking on the phone. I heard the
way she talked about it to her friends, casually, as if the whole

thing was an afterthought on the part of my father. "People say they wouldn't want to live with their mother-in-law alive, how about dead?" she said to Aunt Candace one night on the phone. Candace must have laughed, because I heard my mother use the same line on another one of her friends a few days later. That was the night my father came home late for dinner, a box of gallon paint containers in tow. My mother was boiling pasta. "What, she doesn't like the color of her walls?" she said when she saw the paint. "The dead woman wants her house redecorated. That is rich, Ben. Really."

My father acted as though she wasn't talking, or maybe he truly didn't hear her. He loosened his tie, hung his jacket on the basement doorknob. The water on the stove bubbled over, and my mother picked up the whole pot and dumped it into the sink, noodles and all.

"I don't know what he's trying to prove," she said to me, as he methodically unloaded the box on the landing at the top of the stairs.

In December my mother was busy with the holidays. We were having a New Year's Eve party at our house, something we did every year. My parents had considered canceling the event out of respect for my grandmother, but in the end they didn't. "After all," Aunt Candace said, tapping her red nails on the kitchen counter, "life is for living. And besides, it's more than a month gone by already." My father didn't say anything; things like parties belonged to my mother. This one was going to be bigger than ever; she told me to invite as many friends as I wanted. I pictured myself in one of my mother's dresses, standing in a corner of our living room with Adam Berkman.

In past years they had used the basement; they needed the space with so many guests. She told my father there wasn't enough room without it.

"I should be done down there by then," he said. "We can use

it like always."

"So I should put your mother's name on the invitation?" The way she said it didn't leave room for a reply. My mother had an exclusive on the last word.

I thought she might threaten to cancel the party, but she didn't. She threw herself into the plans with more spirit than ever. She hired a band.

When he was home, my father was in the basement. Evenings, he would change into an old T-shirt and baggy khakis and disappear until it was time for the eleven o'clock news. By the time school let out for winter break, I barely recognized the two rooms. The ping-pong table had been folded into a corner. My grandmother's mahogany wardrobe stood partially on news-papers, as if after refinishing it my father had not had the strength to move it all the way back against the wall. One of the drawers was slightly open, stuffed too full with delicate linens. He had replaced the back of one of her hand-carved chairs; another stood backless, waiting.

I followed the progress of the basement in the mornings, after my father had left for work. I didn't want him to see me down there, to think I was interested, but one day we caught each other. My father, in his suit pants and undershirt, was holding a paint brush. I stood frozen at the foot of the stairs, wondering if I could retrace my steps without drawing his attention, but he looked up and nodded, as if he had been expecting me. "Ilse," he said, "I want to get your opinion on this." He went back to surveying the walls from where he stood in the middle of the room. "I think I've finally got it," he explained. "I wanted to get these pictures just right." He held up a small spiral notebook. "I made some notes of how she had things down in Florida, but I was in such a hurry, I think I missed something."

"I can hardly remember how it was," I said.

"Let me show you what I've done." He waved an arm

ambiguously, the gesture of a conscientious real-estate agent. I followed him through the archway into the smaller of the two rooms, our basement TV room, where he had re-created his mother's bedroom. He had even attached one of her carved headboards to the single bed we kept for guests. "I had to take the basement door off to get this in here." He was pointing to a heavy framed mirror. The crack in the glass made my face too long. I looked away.

"And look at this." He pressed lightly on the double doors of a second wardrobe and they swung open slowly. "I even fixed the hinge. Good as new." He demonstrated a few more times. The *click* and the silence, and then the *click* again, as the doors swung open and he pushed them closed with his index finger, reminded me of a metronome. "All of this has been in the family for years."

He opened the wardrobe drawer. "Here's something you'll like," he said. Inside hung half a dozen "flapper" dresses, heavy beaded gowns of white and silver. "These belonged to your grandmother and her sisters when they lived in the house in Uniontown." He pulled one from the hanger. "All handmade."

I fingered the material, wondering what he expected me to say.

His eyes drifted back through the doorway to the larger room. "It's just too bad about the kitchen," he said.

"What?" I followed his gaze.

"My mother had this tremendous built-in oven unit. I thought of having it ripped out, then this place would have been completely self-sufficient, but . . . ," he trailed off. "Anyway, it's not half bad," he said. "Not bad at all."

"What are you going to do with this when you finish?" I asked. "You know, like rent it out or something?"

"Do." My father pronounced the word not as a question, but as an echo, the way people do when they hear words but have not been listening. He looked at his watch. "It's almost eight thirty. I should get to work." He left me there, in the middle of our windowless recreation room. I sat down on the floor, imagining that I was in a movie, young girl with crazy parents steals a moment of private contemplation. I wondered if he would let me wear one of those dresses to the junior prom. I wondered if it was wrong to think about that, about asking for a dead woman's dress. With its antiques instead of normal basement furniture, its brown shag carpeting and low ceiling, the room reminded me of the showrooms at Ethan Allen or Kaufmann's. It certainly didn't look like a place where anybody lived.

It snowed the whole week between Christmas and New Year's. On Christmas Day, we went to the movies with Uncle Maury and Aunt Candace like we always did; that was what you did in our neighborhood if you didn't celebrate the birth of Christ. That night, Adam Berkman called and asked me to see the same movie the next day. I didn't tell him I had already seen it. I didn't ask him why he had barely spoken to me since we'd had sex, or why he was calling me now. "Sorry I haven't called in a while," he said when we sat down in the theater. "You know."

"We're having a New Year's party," I said, pretending I hadn't heard his apology. I knew enough to know that if I pretended I didn't care, he would believe me. "There's going to be a band." He had his arm around me before the movie even started.

For the rest of the week my mother prepared for the New Year's party while my father puttered in the basement. They were barely speaking to each other, hadn't been in weeks. Even after the basement furniture had long been in place, my father's project had continued. Weekend mornings he left early for flea markets, garage sales, antique shows. He could remember, he explained to me, certain family items his grandfather sold during the lean years of his wallpaper business in the thirties: a marble washstand, the twin to the gold samovar, three butler's tray tables of various sizes. But again and again he came home empty-handed. He was not looking for replacements; he just had a feeling that the originals were out there somewhere, and that he ought to be able to find them.

When he came home from those shopping trips or upstairs from the basement, he would try to tell me stories about his family. He liked to talk about the years before the Depression, when his grandfather's business was booming and there was more money than anyone had ever seen. He told me stories his mother had told him while he was growing up. His stories seemed to come from such large times, the present seemed small and cramped in comparison.

Although I knew I wouldn't, I wanted to ask him what he was doing down in the basement, why it was so important. I could not remember another time like this in our family, when my father had refused to give in to my mother.

On the afternoon of New Year's Eve, our house was transformed. A man in a truck brought seventy fluted champagne glasses. The dining-room rug was lifted for dancing; the tea service shone like new. My mother hadn't said anything about the basement in several days; she simply approached it as a decorator's challenge. The main room of the basement was spotless, and she had covered the tabletops with candles. The smaller room, the one with the bed in it, was dark.

At nine o'clock my mother sparkled in the foyer, greeting guests in her silver jumpsuit. I heard someone tell her she looked like Grace Kelly. I waited in the kitchen for Adam, anticipating how all of this would look through his eyes, how to him I would be Ilse whose parents entertained, Ilse who could serve her friends champagne in front of her own parents, certainly not Ilse whose father refinished furniture while her mother sulked upstairs.

From the kitchen I could hear some of the things people were saying. Aunt Candace, perched on the living-room sofa, dressed in white from head to toe, was explaining to the president of the local Bar Association that he simply *must* see the basement before he left, as if my father's project marked the beginning of a new trend in decorating. People were impressed with what my mother had managed to do with all those candles. *All those old things,* someone said, and I was not sure the words were meant as praise.

Just before midnight, Adam asked me if I wanted to get some air. We walked to his car, holding hands. All evening I had been thinking that I didn't even know if I liked him, but it didn't matter. We drove around for about twenty minutes, weaving our way slowly around the neighborhood, not really talking. I was thinking about sex, wondering if that was why he wanted to leave the party, but he seemed interested in driving. We shared a cigarette, I fiddled with the car radio. "I think we should see more of each other," Adam said. "You know, even when school starts again." He tossed the cigarette butt out the window.

I knew this was what I was supposed to want, but I wished I were somewhere else.

Before I could say anything, we pulled back onto our street and I could see the brilliant light reflecting in the snow. At first I thought it was just the lights from the windows of our house, from the party. And then I saw the people on the lawn and—I don't know why—I thought, *My mother must have planned a scavenger hunt.* In the seconds before I saw the fire engines, I could almost see the well-dressed guests digging in snowdrifts for clues. And then we were close enough to see that the house was burning, and I told Adam to stop the car. I ran. People were everywhere, just like at a fire drill, all over the lawn, in the street, on the Goldberg's front porch. Our house was burning from the bottom up.

I walked around the cluster of people on the sidewalk until I saw my father; he was talking to a fire fighter with a notepad, telling him the story, how in the confusion leading up to midnight a candle must have been knocked over in the basement, somewhere just under the stairs. Before anyone realized what was going on, the flames started and my father had led everyone outside. He couldn't put it out by himself, but the fire department came, and everything was under control. Then he saw me and he told me that our house was not really burning down, it just looked like it. Everything was under control, he kept saying to me. "It looks worse than it is," he said.

The fireman nodded. "They've already contained it."

"Where's Mom?"

My father pointed to the Goldberg's porch. "She's fine. Why don't you go wait up there, too?"

My mother was just to the side of where the other women were standing, as if space were required to watch something as momentous as the burning of your house. An unfamiliar pink sweater was draped over her narrow shoulders. Her eyes were bright, and she looked serene. Before my mother saw me, I saw it. In the palm of her right hand she held her mother's gold locket; the fingers of her other hand formed a tight fist.

In the seconds before she turned to me I could see my mother arrange her face, close her fingers around the locket, and I knew. When Adam found me at the edge of the porch, I asked him to go home.

We slept that night at Aunt Candace and Uncle Maury's. When I woke up the next morning, we went home to survey the damage. The basement stairs were hollow and we couldn't go down there without a ladder. My mother tied back her hair and set to work cleaning up from the party, as if nothing had happened. I followed my father out the side door, into the driveway.

"At least everyone got out safely," my father said, looking at the places where the basement windows had cracked. I wanted to tell my father I was sorry about what had happened, but I didn't know how. So I went inside to call Adam Berkman, and asked him to pick me up. Then I stood with my father in the driveway, where the heat from the flames had melted the snow into pools of oily water, thinking about how I would describe the damage to Adam. By the time he pulled up, the night before was already fading into versions of a story that would be easier to tell, a family story about a ball of fire lighting the sky orange on the last day of the year, the day my mother filled the house with candles to mark our family forging ahead into a new decade. I was my mother's daughter, and I believed that what I knew wasn't important, not as important as what I appeared to know.

Siobhan Dowd, program director of PEN American Center's Freedom-to-Write Committee, writes this column regularly, alerting readers to the plight of writers around the world who deserve our awareness and our writing action.

Writer Detained: Ma Thida
by Siobhan Dowd

Western governments and companies should think twice before treating last year's release of Daw Aung San Suu Kyi as a green light for increased rapprochement and trade with Burma. The junta which governs the country still boasts one of the worst human rights records in southeast Asia: many of Daw Aung San Suu Kyi's colleagues in the National League for Democracy, the party which won the 1990 elections, remain imprisoned in conditions that are dire; civil liberties are virtually nonexistent; and all dissent is silenced—newspapers remain subject to prior restraint and hundreds of book titles, including those by Daw Aung San Suu Kyi, are still banned. At least ten writ-

Ma Thida

ers remain jailed for nothing other than their writings and opinions.

Ma Thida, a campaign assistant of Daw Aung San Suu Kyi, is the writer serving the harshest prison term in Burma or elsewhere in the world. In 1988, in a poem protesting the martial law imposed that year, she wrote, "The distribution of three lines of poetry can earn you a twenty-year sentence." Five years later, her assessment proved deadly accurate: she was sentenced to just that term and is not due for release until 2013. Recent reports about her dire state of health suggest that, for all her youth (she is twenty-nine), her chances of surviving her sentence are remote.

A native of Rangoon, Ma Thida started medical school when she was a mere sixteen years old. At nineteen her first short story, "In the Shade of an Indian Almond Tree," was published. She pursued both professions avidly and, by 1988, the year Burma's democracy movement flourished, she had had some sixty stories published and was close to being qualified as a doctor. She put both callings on hold, however, in order to devote herself to the National League for Democracy, headed by Daw Aung San Suu Kyi. Ma Thida registered new members, distributed information, and soon became so valued by the party that she was promoted to Information Officer. Part of the inner circle, she accompanied Suu Kyi on her extensive travels around the countryside.

In July 1989, Daw Aung San Suu Kyi's electioneering was halted by the arrests of top NLD members and by Suu Kyi herself being placed under house arrest. Ma Thida, probably because of her youth, was not arrested. She became a trainee editor for two pro-democracy magazines. When the universities reopened in November, she returned to medical school, qualifying in September 1990. She also returned to her writing, but well over half of the material she submitted for publication was banned.

Although the country was by now in the harsh grip of the military, Ma Thida went on quietly supporting the cause of democracy. She remained fiercely loyal to Daw Aung San Suu Kyi throughout splits in the NLD. She also documented human-rights abuses, including severe censorship, and wrote articles about her findings, usually under a pseudonym. Simultaneously, she addressed some of the country's social ills, focusing on the unhappy lot of Burmese women. Many of her stories attack the lack of sensible gynecological advice available and attempt to strike down taboos surrounding the subject. In *Hard Labour,* for instance, a medical student relates the tragic lives of three women who have had a series of life-threatening pregnancies. One of them, a recent widow, has had ten pregnancies:

> Those of us who considered ourselves quite knowledgeable, and who had intended to prescribe the previously taboo treatment of "sterilization," now realized it was too late. Too late, much too late, for us to be using this word now. We knew that for this woman with her wretched life and pain it would be forever too late. So, out of our concern and embarrassment, the word we had always been reluctant to utter remained unspoken.

At the time of her arrest, Ma Thida was running a women's clinic one day a week at a monastery in North Rangoon and had secured funding for another clinic for ex-prisoners traumatized by the abuses they suffered during captivity. "These projects were typical of Ma Thida," reports a British friend of hers, Anna Allott. "She was always trying to find ways to help people."

Ma Thida had just finished her first novel, *The Sunflower,* which had been approved for publication. The story's heroine was based on Daw Aung San Suu Kyi and the text contained flashbacks, double-meanings, and symbols, to disguise the true subject matter and thus bypass the censors. After her arrest, publication was abruptly halted.

In the summer of 1993, the axe fell; her house was searched in July, many of her papers were seized, and she was questioned for twenty hours. She was arrested a few days later and charged with "endangering public peace, having contact with illegal organizations, and distributing unlawful literature." Her trial was postponed twice because so many people crowded outside the court, eager to observe. It was held at last within the walls of Insein jail where she was detained. Her twenty-year sentence was announced that October.

Ever more grave reports about her health worry her friends and colleagues, who now fear for her life. The news as of last August was that she was to undergo an operation for "ovarian tumors."

"She was always a diminutive, frail woman," says Allott, and adds, as if by way of hope, "She *is* a devout Buddhist, and though an unassuming person, she has a will of iron."

Letters on behalf of Ma Thida should be sent to:

His Excellency General Than Shwe, Chairman
State Law and Order Restoration Council
c/o Ministry of Defense
Signal Pagoda Road
Yangon UNION OF MYANMAR

*In memory of the novelist **Ken Saro-Wiwa**, who was executed by
Nigerian authorities on Friday, November 10, 1995*

I profiled the case of Ken Saro-Wiwa for *Glimmer Train* in issue thirteen, Winter 1995. The piece was inspired by my having met him shortly before his May 1994 arrest. He was a slight, spry man, with prematurely whitened curls, a quiet dignity, and a gently humorous  smile. As he talked his eyes lit up, his hands moved gracefully.

An ardent champion of minority rights and a stern critic of oil pollution by multinationals, he tried to explain to me why he did what he did. "I just have to," he concluded, as if mystified himself by the underlying reasons. "But if you go back," I said, "you will surely be arrested sooner or later." (He had already had several run-ins with successive military governments.) "I have to go back anyway," he replied. "Even if they kill me. It is my country." At the time, I thought his statement hyperbolic— surely this much-loved literary figure had too devoted and extensive a following for him to be dispatched in such a manner? How wrong I was.

He left, handing me an eloquent piece he had written about oil pollution in his home, Ogoniland, in Nigeria's south. I tried to get it published in the *New York Times,* but without success. News of his arrest soon followed. His trial was denounced as a travesty the world over, and his death sentence sparked presidential condemnation and threats that the World Bank would withdraw a loan. Shell, the Dutch/UK oil company that Ken said had polluted his homeland beyond recognition, refused to intervene until the eleventh hour, when it announced it had sent a letter asking for clemency; the action proved too little, too late. He was hung the next day.

His death has at least ensured that the front pages of the world press are filled with mentions of the plight of his beloved Ogoniland; the Commonwealth has expelled Nigeria, the first country ever to be thus penalized, and the United States has recalled its ambassador.

I cannot think of his last moments without a terrible chill; all of us in the human-rights community feel keenly our failure to prevent his death. But our dejection should not discourage us from continuing our work; Ken would not want it so. And, had we watched silently while he was killed, Nigeria's military leaders would probably feel free to execute countless more of its critics. Now at least they have gotten the message.

David Huddle

They tell me this is me. I think the kid looks suspiciously
like my older brother. On the other hand, something about
the shoes is familiar. And look at this austere bench, this
black background! No wonder the little guy's smile is
tentative. With that dark universe just about to swallow him
up, even this much of a grin was an act of heroism.

David Huddle's most recent book is *Tenorman*, a novella published by
Chronicle Books in 1995. He teaches at the University of Vermont and the
Bread Loaf School of English.

DAVID HUDDLE
The Story of a Million Years

*I*f he could, Jimmy would be unfaithful to me. He can't seem to manage it. I imagine that he feels terrible for what he thinks of as his various infidelities to me. It is true that now and then he has made a ruckus of unfaithfulness—there was the time he confessed his longtime love to Marcy, my best friend. But being a rake is only what Jimmy thinks he wants to be. The truth is that he wants to be what he is, a house husband—Mr. Stay-at-Home-and-Tend-to-Things.

Plenty of the other kind of man chased me when I was in nursing school. These were U.Va. med students who tried to give us nursing students the impression that they were going to be fabulous husbands, hard-working family men with good homes in the suburbs. Meanwhile they were screwing every-thing in sight—especially nursing students who hoped to marry doctors.

In our family, I am the one who brings in most of the income, the one who pays the bills, the one who decides when we trade cars, and so on. Jimmy teaches part-time at the community college, and he does some freelance journalism, but what he mostly does, in addition to spending time with our kids, is grocery shopping, cooking, laundry, and house cleaning.

Long before he thought about getting married, long before he

Glimmer Train Stories, Issue 18, Spring 1996
© 1996 David Huddle

met me, Jimmy was a husband. He is incorrigibly domestic, which has always made him very dear to me. It was for that married quality that I fell in love with him and married him. I know Jimmy better than he can ever know himself. I even know better than to explain some of the things I know to him—such as why he still spends so much time listening to A.B.C.'s crazy ideas.

Marcy and I have known Allen Crandall since we were all in high school. His middle name's Ballston, which is why everybody calls him A.B.C. He's like a project she and I have worked on for all these years. Jimmy was in A.B.C.'s first-year dormitory at U.Va. When he came into the picture, Marcy and I could never decide if we should work on him as part of the project or if he actually was helping us with the A.B.C. project. Jimmy always tells me how much he can't stand A.B.C., how despicable A.B.C.'s behavior is, and so on. Jimmy has no idea how much he needs A.B.C. He behaves as if Marcy and I are forcing him to be A.B.C.'s buddy.

One night about a year ago, A.B.C. told Marcy, Jimmy, and me this dream he had. It wasn't exactly a dream of flying, because there was some kind of mode of transportation to which he was connected, as if he were strapped to the nose of a plane, the prow of a ship, the engine of a train. What the thing was that propelled him forward he couldn't really see. His movement was so vigorous that the speed wasn't what he was most aware of in the dream. It was more his mastery of space; the mountains and cities and river valleys through which he moved were instruments that he found he could play as his mood inspired him. Exposed to the wind, the heat, the rain, the cold, darkness and light, he found that they, too, were his—the elements belonged to him and gave him pleasure.

"It was a *very* good dream," A.B.C. purred in that sly way of his that always makes me want to give him a quick smack across his face. But then he explained that he had less and less control of both the speed and the direction of his movement. Finally whatever the thing was that had picked him up and given him this incredible ride, raised him to a great height above the earth, then sent him careening downward at an insane velocity. A.B.C. hit the earth with a devastating impact. But then he saw that he wasn't harmed at all. He remembered thinking to himself, "How come I'm not dead yet?" He felt good. He was sitting on a plain of mown grass. But he had no more extraordinary powers of movement. When he stood up and walked across the grass, he was merely walking.

A.B.C. said he told us his dream because he wanted us to help him figure out what it meant. "Analyze it for me, please," he said, very smugly, as if he would be judging our analytical powers through this exercise. I think he really told it because it was a dream that testified to the power he claims as his. Not only does A.B.C. do most of what he wants to do whenever he wants to do it, he also wants to be loved for being just that way. Don't ask me why. Women don't want to move through their lives the way men do, pushing through a crowd of people to get where they think they want to go.

"It's a little boy's dream, A.B.C.," I told him, but he ignored me. Or he acted like he was ignoring me. I know he pays attention to what I say, mostly because I don't say much around him. So I watched Jimmy while A.B.C. talked about this dream. Jimmy sat forward in his chair. I could tell he didn't quite understand the dream, but he knew he liked it. He knew it connected to something inside himself. He asked A.B.C. questions. Long after Marcy and I had gone to the kitchen to fix some tea for ourselves, he and A.B.C. went on talking about the silly dream.

But like Jimmy, I am not always in touch with all of my feelings about the man. Five or six years ago, the Crandalls and the Ragos hired ourselves a couple of American University girls to look after our kids, all of them over at the Crandalls' house. The four of us drove our car down to Key West for a vacation in March. When we were in college, we never took those road trips that everybody else took at spring break. Back then A.B.C. was playing baseball for U.Va., and so he wasn't available to go. Marcy and I and Jimmy usually ended up hanging around Charlottesville, pretending to study. So this trip was going to be a spring break for grown-ups. On the drive down there, we were all four really enjoying ourselves, singing along with the radio, stopping to eat at these corny little roadside places left over from the fifties.

Wouldn't you know, something would go wrong. When we got to the motel, we called home and found out that three of our four girls had come down with the flu. It was serious stuff that year—they were calling it the California Flu, because a couple of kids out there had actually died from it—high fevers, throwing up, complete exhaustion, all that. So we checked out of the motel an hour after we'd checked in. We put Jimmy and Marcy—the main kid-raising parent from each family—on a plane back to Dulles. A.B.C. and I started driving the car north. No big deal, we've all known each other forever. Besides, all four of us understand that I have a low tolerance for A.B.C.'s ways. "Ute doesn't go for A.B.C.'s bullshit," is what Jimmy loves to tell people when he's telling them about his hero.

Driving up through Florida, A.B.C. and I don't have much to say to each other. Even though it's our car, A.B.C. is at the wheel. I didn't feel like arguing with him when he asked for the keys, but it started me out in a nasty frame of mind. We're both pissed that our vacation is ruined, the weather is hot, and all we've got to look forward to is miles and miles of interstate.

After we cross up into Georgia, the weather cools down, and I realize we've been driving in almost complete silence. "Put a little music into this show, Allen," I say. I turn on the car radio and tune in a station. A.B.C. gives me a feeble grin, like he wishes we were having a better time, too, but he doesn't have very high hopes for it.

All of a sudden this radio station is playing Ray Charles tunes from back in the sixties, "What'd I Say" and "I Got a Woman" and "Hit the Road, Jack." It's a crazy thing, but a long time ago at mixers or frat parties or wherever one of those songs would come along, if there was dancing to be done, A.B.C. would find me or I would find him, and we'd dance like nothing you've ever seen. When the song was over, I'd be blushing like I'd just had sex with the man out there on the floor. The way we danced, sometimes it was pretty close to that. I can't account for it—it was just the way things were. In just about every other way, he and I had no use for each other. But to that music, I had to dance with A.B.C., and he had to dance with me. I know he's vain; I know he can't think about anybody but himself; I know he's a liar and a cheat. I hate him for all those things—except when Ray Charles starts singing and I need the right man to dance with me. Marcy and Jimmy kidded us and each other about it, but they didn't like it. A.B.C. and I didn't blame them.

So we're driving up the interstate, the weather's just turned nice, and we're hearing Ray doing "You Are My Sunshine" in that way that turns A.B.C. and me on every time we hear it. He looks over at me and winks. I look back at him and raise my eyebrows. We're bopping our heads, sliding our shoulders, and snapping our fingers. We're a couple of kids out on the road with nothing but good times coming to us. It's bad, I know it is. I need to tell him, "Don't be thinking whatever it is that you're thinking, A.B.C.," but I don't tell him. The thrill doesn't come into me so much anymore. This afternoon I haven't gone looking for it, but now that it's here, along with a cool wind in my hair and Ray singing, "The other night, dear, while I lay sleeping...," I'm not going to turn it off. I glance over at A.B.C. and push the hair out of my eyes.

A.B.C. and I take our lunch at the Peach Pit Bar-B-Q in northern Georgia. Things are different between us. He's asking me questions, and I'm answering him. I'm enjoying answering him. He says he's amazed to find out that I can actually speak more than a couple of sentences at a time. It's true, I don't have much to say in most circumstances, especially social occasions—and most especially to him. But I've always had lots to say to Marcy, and every now and then Jimmy finds a way to get me talking. I tell A.B.C. that I actually like talking, it's just that he's never shown any interest in what I might have to say. He says that's not true. I tell him that he knows it is true. We stuff ourselves with barbecue and coleslaw and french fries. Then we're grinning at each other and moaning about how full we are as we stand up and head for the cashier's counter.

So there's a little buzz in the air between us as we're moving up through South Carolina. A.B.C. has given me the wheel—which is almost beyond remarkable; so far as I know he's never let Marcy drive him anywhere, in his car or hers. We've taken the western corridor toward home, Interstate 77, and as we come up into North Carolina, the sky is looking pretty strange way up ahead of us. A.B.C. nods at it, then looks at me. I shrug.

An hour later, we're in a blizzard. In this one day we've gone from weather that would have let us swim and sunbathe on the beach in Florida, to slick roads and low visibility in the mountains of western North Carolina. "What the fuck?" A.B.C. shouts at the windshield. I think it's just about the same question I've got on my mind. A Mayflower moving van passes us, blinds us, and nearly blows us off the road.

So A.B.C. and I sit in the parking lot of the Holiday Inn just outside Mount Airy, North Carolina, and the topic of discussion is one room or two. It's not an argument, and we're not mad at each other. Crazy as it is, we're trying to figure how to play it for Jimmy and Marcy. A.B.C. says it doesn't make any difference to him, but I'm guessing he doesn't want to be alone, either. Something about the snow: coming down like this in the springtime, it's scary beyond just bad road conditions.

We take two rooms next to each other on the ground floor. We each unpack what we need and stash it. Then I go to A.B.C.'s room where I dial the Crandalls' number at home to tell them what's what and to find out how things are there. There's a light snow in the D.C. area, so the crazy blizzard in North Carolina makes sense to them. Marcy is on the phone in Jenny's room, where the girls are holed up in their sickbeds, and Jimmy is on the phone downstairs in the kitchen. He's on his way over to our house. I don't like talking on the phone to the two of them. So I put A.B.C. on the line and listen to him taking pains to let them know we've taken the two rooms. They go on telling him about the girls, who are definitely sick as dogs but who don't seem likely to die. They exchange good-byes, take cares, and see you tomorrows. When he sets the receiver down, A.B.C. and I are sitting opposite each other on the beds with the little bedside-phone cabinet between us. I sit there, and he sits there. I can't bring myself to look him in the eye. I don't think he's looking straight at me either. This moment goes on too long before A.B.C. finally says, "Dinner, U."

"Dinner, Allen," I say, too. I sound like a zombie. "Zombie dinner," I say. When A.B.C. asks me what the hell I'm talking about, I shake my head and give him a little grimace. I don't bother changing clothes. I sit in my zombie pose while A.B.C. brushes his teeth.

I get my wish in the Holiday Inn dining room—a dinner fit for zombies. I can't imagine what I was thinking to have ordered the seafood stir-fry; on the other hand, I can't imagine what I could have ordered in this place that I would have liked. A.B.C. doesn't finish his beef tournedos, which means they must be gruesome. We don't talk about it, though; the unacceptable food is just this depressing understanding between us. Through the floor-to-ceiling restaurant windows we watch the snow floating down outside; they've got spotlights on outside, so that the huge flakes look like swarms of monster moths swirling against a black background. It's the third week of March, nearly cherry-blossom time in D.C.

"What time is it?" I ask A.B.C.

"Quarter of eight." His voice has this amused and exhausted and exasperated and slightly curious tone to it. I understand him. When we were roommates in nursing school, Marcy used to say that I didn't know nearly as much about what people were thinking as I thought I did. What she didn't understand was that quiet people learn to pay attention to things like the tone of voice somebody uses. In this case A.B.C. is telling me what time it is, but he's actually asking, "Isn't this a hell of a mess?" and, "What are we going to do with all these hours ahead of us?"

"Let's do dessert," I say. "Holiday Inn has decent desserts."

"What idiot told you that, U.? Holiday Inn is the enemy of every variety and nationality of food. Holiday Inn has decent nothing whatsoever, except maybe forks and spoons."

So we order the brownie à la mode for him, the carrot cake for me. They're edible, which cheers us a bit. Over the decaf, we're sitting back in our chairs, taking stock, looking at the other diners who are glancing back at us. A.B.C. says they're figuring us for a married couple. He's right about that, it's evident from the way they let their eyes just skim across us, checking us off their nothing-remarkable-there lists. Or maybe that's just the way I'm seeing all the other married couples in there. There's nobody in the whole dining room who looks like I'd want to talk to them for longer than about three minutes.

I find myself telling A.B.C. about my spring break my senior year of nursing school. Jimmy's parents had made him come home to help with painting the family's summer place. Marcy hadn't wanted to leave Charlottesville, and I was sick of hanging out down there. So on a last-minute whim, I'd gone to New York with a couple of friends, Nancy Parks and Margaret Atwater. These were classmates of mine and Marcy's, girls we liked but didn't know all that well. The price Marcy and I paid for being such good friends with each other was that we didn't develop really close friendships with other girls. Nancy and Margaret were the same way, close to each other but more like friendly acquaintances with everybody else. The two pairs of friends appreciated each other even if we weren't all that intimate. Nancy and Margaret had these guys they knew from high school who had an apartment in the city and who would let us sleep on the floor and the sofa of their living room. It was all kind of kinky and spontaneous and what-the-heck-it'll-work-out-fine.

We got to the city on the afternoon of March the seventeenth, Saint Patrick's day. It was like driving into a fraternity party attended by about three million people. In spite of all the craziness in the streets, we did find the building, we did get the car parked, we did get our stuff stashed inside the guys' apartment, we did get ourselves gussied up and back out on the town for the revelry. I couldn't seem to take everything in; it was all just a blur of the wildest confusion. I'd never been to New York before and certainly never imagined that a whole city could turn into one big drinking party. Nancy and Margaret and I, with these two guys leading us through the crowds from one bar to another, got used to screaming at each other if we had to communicate or making frantic signals across a bunch of people. That seemed like fun for a while, but then my voice got too scratchy to be able to scream any more. The signals we made to each other were just *I'm nervous* and *Isn't this crazy?* and *Should we or shouldn't we?* signals. We all got tired of doing them.

We were in a bar called Dolan's, a big cozy room with Celtic music coming through the speakers and lots of dark wood and pictures of old-time football and baseball players and boxers on the walls. Of course Dolan's was so packed with human bodies that just standing in one place was almost a sexual experience. Nobody'd said so, but Dolan's seemed to be where we were settling in for the evening. I'd lost track of the guys who'd brought us there, but I could see Margaret across the way, and I thought I heard Nancy's high-pitched laugh over near the bar behind me. Going through the motions of talking with some guy in a suit, I was trying to figure out just how drunk I was, but that was difficult because the world around me was drunk, too.

At U.Va., hanging out with Jimmy and Marcy and A.B.C., I had gotten used to drinking a lot on weekends and even during the week on occasion. I had a reputation for being able to hold my booze—which essentially meant that when Marcy was puking in the bushes or the trash can in our room, I was just keeping all that stuff in my system so that I could feel terrible the next morning.

I couldn't understand the guy I was talking to, and I know he couldn't understand me—I wasn't even certain the noises I was making were words or sentences—but it was pleasant enough to stand there with him making sounds to each other. When he shouted an offer to get me another drink I shouted back *sure*. And when he carried it back through the crowd to me, I was talking to another guy. I took the drink and said thank you and was aware of that guy being swept back away from me and the new guy as if he'd gotten caught in a mud slide.

It went on that way. I was even having what I might have called fun, except it was such a peculiar variety of fun, just standing in a swarm of people, making noises now and then, nodding, smiling, sipping my drink, spacing out and watching all these strangers in an absent-minded kind of way. I was of course occasionally having to fend off a guy's hand from my ass or dodge around a guy who wanted to brush his triceps against my boobs, but these maneuvers by the guys and by me were more friendly than hostile. I shouted to the guy I was talking to at the moment to ask him what time it was, and he shouted back, "What difference does it make?" I realized he was right, it didn't matter. So I raised my glass to him, and we toasted time thrown out the window. It was about then that I realized I wasn't seeing

Margaret, and I wasn't hearing Nancy. The guys who'd brought us to the place had long since disappeared; I couldn't even remember what they looked like now.

I didn't panic. I figured Margaret or Nancy would turn up before too long. There were so many people around, the bar was such a cheerful place, that I knew there wasn't anything to be frightened of. I had my little party purse right there with me with my makeup, my ID card, and a twenty-dollar bill in it. But something in the back of my brain clicked on and instructed me not to get any drunker than I was.

One part of my consciousness went on with the partying. Another part went off into a quiet room and started calculating. It was possible that Margaret and Nancy had gone in separate directions, each figuring that the other would stick with me. Or it could have been the case that they figured I could look after myself. And I could; I was a big girl; I could drive and vote and get a job and hold my booze and get married and have sex and make babies and do anything else I felt like doing. What I couldn't do was remember the address of the apartment where we were staying. This was a troublesome piece of forgetting. Actually, I couldn't remember if I'd ever known the address— Nancy and Margaret had known it, and so it had never seemed necessary for me to know it. I didn't think I could remember how to get back to that building. I thought that if I had plenty of time to look for it in daylight, I could probably find it because I remembered what it looked like. It had to be within walking distance of Dolan's because we'd walked here, though we'd stopped at half a dozen bars along the way. What my brain was telling me was that I didn't want to be out on the street looking for that building in the early morning hours.

When I went to a phone booth to see if I could get a number and maybe an address for one of the guys in that apartment, I realized that I wasn't certain of either of their last names. There was a Kevin and a Bernie. And I thought one of them might have been a Williams or a Wiggins. The New York Telephone Company can't do much for you if all you've got is a Kevin and a Bernie with one of them maybe being named Williams or Wiggins.

Guys had been buying me drinks all night; I kept on letting that happen. And I kept circulating, because after I'd talked with one guy long enough, he'd start touching me, usually just a pat on the shoulder, a touch on the wrist, a light hand at the small of my back. That was the signal for me to excuse myself and move on. I wasn't angry at being touched that way, I just knew I didn't want to give anybody the idea that I might sleep with him that evening.

I paced myself carefully. Drunk when I figured out the situation, I restricted myself to sipping throughout the rest of the evening. So I managed to sober up gradually as the hours went by.

The crowd thinned out. I didn't know what time it was, but I figured it must be around two. One of the problems with the thinning out was that the male-to-female ratio went up drastically. The majority of the males who were left were what Jimmy would have called shit-faced. In another hour there were half a dozen shit-faces slumped at the bar; I was the only female in the whole place, and there were only a couple of guys I felt safe talking to. One of them was the bartender.

I still didn't panic. False sense of security, I guess. I kept reminding myself that I was a grown-up, I had my wits about me, I was healthy, I'd even assisted during cardiovascular surgery and had my hands inside somebody's chest a fraction of an inch away from a beating human heart. Surely I could manage to get through a few hours until it was daylight. Then I could go out on the street and look for the place where I was staying.

"Closing time, folks," the bartender announced. The guy I'd been talking to asked me if I needed a place to stay. When I shook my head no, he grinned at me, told me it had been real, and left. Funny, because I had thought he might try to persuade me; I had even considered bargaining with him for a place on a sofa if he had one.

One by one and none too steadily, the shit-faces made their way out. When the last one was gone, I kept sitting at the bar. The bartender was washing a load of glasses. I remember thinking, so now it's down to me and him. It occurred to me that I had put a fair portion of my fate in his hands. He looked up at me and lifted his eyebrows. "Well, now, little lady," he said.

"Can I talk to you?" I asked him.

"Sure you can," he said. "But first let me lock this door so we don't get any more drunks wandering in here." When he walked out from behind the bar to the main entrance and bolted it shut, I figured that either I was in for big trouble or I was okay. This was a barrel-chested guy, mid-thirties, with a ponytail and a handlebar moustache. He had on a yellow, button-down oxford shirt that somebody had ironed meticulously—I figured a wife or a girlfriend. Walking back toward me, he fished a pack of cigarettes out of his shirt pocket, shook one out, and lit it as he sat down on the bar stool next to me. "So what's the story?" he asked me.

I told him.

He sat with his head propped on his hand, smoking and now and then asking me a question like what the building looked like and what else I remembered about the street and how we got here. "So what are you gonna do?" he finally asked me.

"When it gets daylight, I'm going out there to look for the place," I told him.

He looked at me steadily.

"I think I can find it," I said.

"How about some coffee?" he said.

He fixed a pot, and while it was brewing I helped him put the chairs up on the tables. Then we sat at the bar drinking his coffee and chatting. Gregory Bates was his name. This guy had a way about him of just calmly being there, not making me feel like he was doing me a favor—which he most definitely was doing. And both of us got absorbed in our conversation. He liked talking about how it was to work in that bar. Since I'd just paid a lot of attention to how things happened in this evening at Dolan's, I was interested in how Gregory saw it all from behind the bar. And he was interested in nursing. He said he sometimes even thought about going to nursing school. At the time, I believed him about that; nowadays, I think he was probably just trying to make me feel at ease. At any rate, we were talking so intently and we were in such a strange little unit of time that we went off into our own world there for a while. When I happened to follow Gregory's eyes and glance back behind me to the windows, it had become broad daylight.

"Why didn't you tell me it was light outside?" I yelled at him. I was gleeful beyond what anybody could have understood. I felt

136   *Glimmer Train Stories*

like a prisoner who'd been set free.

Gregory just shrugged and grinned. "Want me to help you find this place you're staying?" he asked me. And I took him up on his offer. He had an idea of which neighborhood this apartment building was in. Sure enough, we walked up the street a couple of blocks, over one block, and down another, and there it was. Gregory said so long, he'd better be getting over to his place to catch up on his sleep. I kissed him on his handlebar moustache, thanked him, and watched him walk away. That was when I realized something about Gregory Bates as certainly as if he'd whispered it to me himself: nobody else had ironed that yellow shirt for him, he'd ironed it for himself. I shook my head and wondered why in the world such a piece of knowledge as that would come to me. Then I went into the foyer of the building and faced a bank of buttons for the doorbell–intercom system.

It was no problem finding Kevin Wilson on the little tag beside the button for #3F. I had my finger poised to push that button when I reminded myself that it was probably not much past six in the morning. This seems strange to me now, when I think about it, but I decided not to bother Kevin and Bernie and Nancy and Margaret in the apartment so early in the day. I mean, given the fact that they had abandoned me for the evening, I should have set off fireworks and sirens to wake them all up. But for some reason I had this sweetness in me, sort of like Gregory's calmness. I thought to myself, I can let them sleep; they've been up partying. They're exhausted, and I'm safe now. There's no reason why I can't give them more time to sleep.

So I sat down on the floor of the foyer and let my head rest back against the wall. Like a propped-up Raggedy Ann doll, I let my legs stretch out in front of me. And I went to sleep. It was not a cat nap. I went way down into sleep. I think I even did some quite vivid dreaming, though I wasn't able to remember any of the dreams. What woke me was a guy in a suit standing over me in the foyer, looking down with a smile, and saying, "Good morning, Sleeping Beauty. Happy Day-After-Saint-Patrick's-Day."

After that, the only thing that happened was that I rang the doorbell and got someone to buzz me in. They were all four a little pissed at me for waking them even at that time of day, which was a bit after seven. Nancy and Margaret hadn't been at all worried about me; it hadn't occurred to them that I wouldn't have remembered where we were staying. Margaret had seen me talking with this "stud," as she called him, and figured I'd spent the rest of the evening with him. I couldn't even remember which guy I'd talked to that they might have considered a "stud." The only guy I'd met all night that I had any clear memory of was Gregory, and he and I hadn't exchanged a word until after everybody else was out of the bar.

A.B.C. is disappointed that that's the end of my story. It's not exactly, but I have trouble getting across to him what it was that had stuck with me from that evening and made me remember it. It was that crazy little bit of sweetness that came into me in the foyer when I was standing there all by myself with my finger about to press the doorbell, when I knew I was safe, and I decided not to disturb the sleepers. That was the closest I'll ever come to knowing what it feels like to be one of those highly developed Buddhist monks. It was the only time I've ever had that feeling. When the guy in the suit woke me up, the sweetness had all gone out of me. I felt cranky as an old guard-dog. When I walked up to that third-floor apartment and found out my so-called friends were pissed at me for waking them up and hadn't even been worried about me, I threw a tantrum that shut them all up for the rest of the morning. It was a tantrum that cooled off the friendship between me and Nancy and Margaret for the rest of the time I knew them.

So there was just that one little piece of my life when I was actually a saint. It's funny that I had to go through that whole long journey to get to it—driving up from Charlottesvillle to Manhattan, going through the crazy Saint Patrick's Day evening and even crazier morning in Dolan's. From about 6:03 a.m. until 6:07 a.m. of March 18, 1966, I experienced deep goodness. It was over and done with pretty quickly.

A.B.C. surprises me by being interested in my notion about being good. Actually, it's something I seem to be trying out as I tell it. I've remembered that trip to New York for almost twenty years, but I probably haven't told anybody about it since the afternoon I got back to Charlottesville and gave Marcy a report of my adventures. So it's only in telling A.B.C. about it that my four minutes of goodness got to be such a big deal. But now he wants to know if it registered in my body in any physiological way (it didn't), or if I've thought about it a lot over the years (I haven't), or if—

"Allen, you're trying to make it something out of a book, and it wasn't like that. You could feel the same thing in the next five minutes, and you wouldn't think it was all that unusual—"

"So why are you telling me about it, U.?"

"We're killing time, aren't we?"

"I'm not the one who made such a big deal about it. You're the one who told this whole long story just to get to the part where you took a nap."

This is the way A.B.C. likes to talk to people. It's not really a way he and I have ever talked before, but I've seen him doing these little play-arguments with Jimmy and Marcy. I take it as a sign of his liking me and being interested in what I've told him. But quibbling is not my idea of fun. I shut up and just sit across from him.

He shuts up, too. Which surprises me. A.B.C. is not one to let a conversational opportunity go by. But he seems to be giving a lot of thought to something.

"Speak up, Allen. What's on your mind?"

He clears his throat, but he doesn't meet my eyes. When he

begins talking, his voice is soft. I find I'm having to lean forward over the table to hear him.

"I had this one time," he murmurs, "when I did something okay. I was just now trying to figure if it made me feel that thirty seconds of sainthood you're talking about. I don't think it did. Sandy was about five. It was a Saturday afternoon. Marcy'd gone shopping. I was lying on our bed upstairs, half reading a magazine, half watching some kind of game on the TV. Sandy comes in, very distraught. 'Daddy, what *is* sex?' she asks.

"Something tells me to turn off the TV. So I do. And because she's so agitated, I begin answering her right away—no big deal, what is sex, easy question—and in as calm and soothing a voice as I can get myself to use. 'Well, darling, it's when two people love each other, and they blah, blah, blah.' I don't know what's chewing on Sandy, but I know she's needing an answer. She's needing it bad.

"Of course this is *not* an easy question, no matter who's asking it. So while I'm talking, I'm wondering what in the hell has brought her up here with this on her mind. But I'm also wondering just how to pitch what I'm saying. God knows, I'm no child psychologist. I'm even wishing I had read up on how to tell your kids about sex. I'm talking, but I'm feeling at a complete loss. Ordinarily, of course, I'd say, 'Go ask your mother.' That's not possible now.

"I want to be as straight with Sandy as I can be because my guess is that she's needing what the politicians call 'hard information.' But I can also tell that she's in a vulnerable state. Whatever I tell her will probably register more intensely than it usually would. I don't want to ruin the rest of the kid's life by telling her stuff that's just too damn 'hard' for a five-year-old.

"All this while I'm talking, I've got stuff running through my brain. Like, for instance, I'm aware that I've got my shirt off, and I wish I didn't. I've always been a little self-conscious about having my shirt off around anybody. But it would seem too weird to get up and put it on. I also have my hand rubbing Sandy's back the way I do when I'm trying to make her feel better. It's an old habit from when she was a baby and I could sometimes get her to stop crying by rubbing the top of her back up around her neck and shoulder blades. It feels strange to be rubbing Sandy's back with my shirt off while I'm trying to explain to her about sex. And while I go on spinning out my answer, I'm also remembering that this morning in the kitchen Marcy and I had had this funny conversation about people doing it in odd places. Something she read in the paper brought it up. And I remember that Sandy had been eating her breakfast in there while we were talking. We'd both been aware of her. I was certain our conversation had been rated PG. Meanwhile, of course, I'm going on with my answer, 'Blah, blah, human beings are lucky enough to have this intimate way to express blah, blah, blah—'

" 'Yes, but Daddy, what *is* it really?' she interrupts me.

" 'You mean how does it work?'

" 'Yes.' Sandy's looking me straight in the face, and it's just killing me, the pain I can see she's feeling from whatever she's got on her mind.

"I take a deep breath and tell her, 'The male puts his penis into the female's vagina.' There it is. Sounds silly as hell just to say it. Either I've told her what she needs to know, or I've told her what will ruin her entire life from here on out. Maybe both. I can't tell from her face.

"I'm feeling like the vampire caught out in daylight, and I'm watching Sandy turning it over in her mind. Funny thing—I'm even pissed off at Marcy for not being here when her daughter needs her. And I know that's right out there at the edge of my idiocy, but what can I say? I felt what I felt.

"All of a sudden Sandy's face crumples up, and she's weeping like I'd smacked her. 'Daddy, that's what Kevin just did to me.'

" 'Kevin put his penis in your ...?'

"She's nodding. 'He did!'

"Kevin is the neighbors' son, the same age as Sandy. The two of them have been playing together since before either one of them could even walk. Now I can feel Sandy, in this horrified state, studying my face. She thinks I'm going to punish her or scream at her. Or some other terrible thing is going to happen to her. But at least it's clear to me now what was troubling the poor kid. All of a sudden I feel just so sorry for her. I have the good sense to sit up and pull her close to me and give her a hug, even though I wish I had my shirt on. It doesn't matter. That's actually what I tell her. 'It doesn't matter, darling.' She's really letting the crying go now. That seems just what ought to happen right now. I hold her close and pat her back and get a combination of tears and snot on my bare shoulder.

" 'It's nothing for you to worry about, Sandy,' I say. 'I don't think you and Kevin are far enough along for this to count as actual sex.' I'm hoping this is true even though I can't say that I know anything about it. Can a girl actually lose her virginity at the age of five? Surely to God not! What I know for certain is that no matter what it counts as, Sandy shouldn't have to feel bad about it. 'How did it happen, darling?'

"She goes on to tell me. They were in the bathroom together. They were sort of fooling around. Kevin wanted to try something. Sandy said okay. A whole little parable played out right there in the Plimptons' bathroom. As best I can tell—and I don't press her for explicit details—there was genital-to-genital contact for probably less than a minute. Can a five-year-old boy have an erection? I don't know, but I'm figuring probably not, at least not penetration as it would be for adults. Not the real thing. Maybe I'm just insisting on taking a Walt Disney view of this whole experience. I even ask myself that—am I refusing to see the real horror here? But how can it be horror if it's just kids—little kids!—fooling around?

"As Sandy talks, she calms down. Soon we're back to me lying back on the bed and rubbing her back while she stands there sniffling and telling me the last odds and ends of the story. Finally I've asked her all the questions I want to, and she's told me all she wants to tell. Sandy's getting restless and even a little bored. So I lay some concluding remarks on her. 'Just don't go into the bathroom with Kevin anymore, darling. Okay? Fooling around with him like that is not anything you want to do again, but you'll be fine. Don't you worry.' I tell her maybe it would be better not to play with Kevin any more today. Then I pat her on her back and let her go back downstairs to work on her coloring.

"And I lie there and think about it. I'm tempted to go find Kevin and shake him till his little bones rattle. I figure I'll have to have a word with David Plimpton about this. Sandy had to go through the misery of fessing up to me. Kevin needs a little parental talk, too.

"I hate to admit this to you, U., but I'm lying there feeling just smug as hell. I'm figuring if Sandy had taken that little story to Marcy, Marcy would have exploded. Marcy would have made a hell of a big deal out of it. Which is exactly what Sandy didn't need to have done. I'm actually figuring, now that it's over with, that the way I handled it was maybe my finest hour as a parent. I made the kid understand she hadn't done anything terrible.

"This is the thing about what you're calling 'deep goodness,' U. For me, it's willy-nilly, sometimes good, sometimes a jerk, but either way, it comes out—how should I say?—less than terrific. In this case, I've been good, or about as good as I get. What do I feel? No serenity at the center of the soul for me. Unlike you, I don't get a sweet nap in the foyer of the apartment building. I get half an hour of self-congratulation, followed by the rest of the afternoon losing brain cells watching the football game on TV."

"Are you asking me to feel sorry for you?" I ask him.

"Yeah," he says. He's giving me that old A.B.C. grin. "What's the matter, U.? Don't tell me you're coming up short of compassion for your old pal A.B.C."

Hang out with A.B.C. long enough, you'll want to kill him. I don't give him the satisfaction of an answer. Nothing makes him quite as happy as having me irked at him, anyway. So I grin back at him. "I feel sorry for you, Allen," I tell him in my best fake-sweet voice. We sit there smirking at each other. Then this terrible thing happens. I'm looking at his face, his old face that I've known for I can't count how many years.

I want the man.

I don't have a good reason. If reason had anything to do with it, I'd already be in my room down the hall. I'd be on the phone talking with Jimmy. This thread of desire goes back to Ray Charles on the radio this morning—no, goes way on back years further than that, maybe to the first time I ever danced with him and got a look at how his body worked. I make myself stop staring at his face.

"Time to let this place get along without us, U.," he says, standing up and stretching.

His stretching like that is the killer. My face has to be red. I keep it turned away so he won't notice. I've got nothing to say.

We're paid up and out of there so smoothly it's like we're on a fast train ride to whatever's coming next. We're pacing down the corridors toward our rooms, which are way on the other side of the motel. I'm sober, but I feel the way I used to when I got drunk at parties, as if some crazy, sexual thing were about to happen, and I didn't care. I just wanted to go with it, whatever it was. Usually it was nothing except a lot of people getting drunk and acting stupid.

I've always wondered what it was with me and desire. I can go for months and not feel more than the occasional twinge. I can get to the point where I feel like maybe I'm finally over all that. Or like maybe Jimmy and I have just used up all the desire that was going to come to us, and neither one of us much wants to do it anymore, even though both of us wish we still wanted to do it. Then all of a sudden, it'll be there, real as weather. Mostly it's Jimmy that I want, and mostly when desire drops in on me like this, it's at a time when he and I can do something about it— if Jimmy's in a mood, too. And I can usually get him in a mood if he isn't already. But sometimes it's somebody else, a doctor at the hospital. The ones I work with and admire. Or even this one orderly, a black guy who—what can I say?—just does it for me when it comes to looks. Almost always it's somebody I know pretty well.

What I wonder is if it happens to most women like this— random attacks. I'm used to it. And used to hiding it, waiting it out until it's gone. After I married Jimmy I never acted on it when it was somebody else I wanted. Once I let a doctor kiss me at a staff Christmas party and was so ashamed afterward that I even told Jimmy about it to make sure I wouldn't go any further with that guy. But the thing about it is, when it comes on me like this, I feel like such a slave—to what, I don't know, slave to the invisible master, I guess. I don't know if I'm a freak or if I'm just typical. Guys are supposed to be like this all the time, victims of their glands, wanting sex so bad they can hardly keep their flies up, and so on. I think it's actually women who are the most driven.

I've tried talking to Marcy about this, but she doesn't like the topic. Friend of mine that she is, there are barriers in her that have been up all the years I've known her. "If something happens, it happens," a married girlfriend of mine told me once when I asked her if she really was going to have an affair with this totally inappropriate guy. "I'm not looking for trouble," she said. "But when trouble comes and knocks on my door, I can't be saying I'm not home." What did she mean by that? I asked her, but she just gave me a shrug and this bitter little smile. Now I know. Walking with A.B.C. down this last corridor toward our rooms, I give my head a shake. I feel like trouble is knocking at my door, and I'm at home, I'm at home, I'm at home.

"My place or yours?" he says when we arrive at the side-by-side doors. His physical presence is radiological. I'm not looking at him, but I'm registering the shape of his body shimmering right beside me.

"Not funny," I say, putting my key in the lock and pushing the door open. I'm hoping I can walk my way through this. I may have the fever, but that doesn't mean he has to know it. I can just do what I'd ordinarily do, and he won't know the difference.

"What's up, U? Something happening here? Please clue in your old pal Allen."

He's just standing beside my door. I step inside and turn to him, but I can't raise my eyes to his. *Close the door!* my mind is shouting. *Just close the door!* But some other voice is quietly saying, *You can't close the door in his face.*

The instant hovers. Then he steps inside. I take a step back but still stand there facing him—a short dance. A.B.C. reaches back to the door behind him. He pushes it slowly, watching me. I meet his eyes now. He eases the door shut so that even though I know it's coming, the click of the latch startles me.

The room isn't totally dark. Light seeps in around the curtain of the window at the opposite side of the room. I know I need to say something, need just to make a little conversation to snap everything back to normal. But the words aren't coming. While I stand here facing A.B.C., my eyes adjust to the dark; it becomes lighter and lighter shades of gray that let me gradually make out details of his face. It's like standing in a black-and-white photograph while it's developing.

"We can turn on the light, U.," he murmurs.

"Turn it on then," I say.

"You turn it on," he says.

Neither of us moves. We stand like that, facing each other.

He raises an arm and extends it across the space between us and touches my forearm, just above the elbow. He lets his fingers stay there on the skin of my arm long enough for me to look down at them.

Then A.B.C. and I are into it, what was coming to us sure as the clock striking midnight. We're nearly lunging at each other's mouths. We're crude and awkward—I've probably cut the inside of my lip banging it against A.B.C.'s teeth. And he can't decide whether he wants to undress me or himself, so that I don't know which way I'm supposed to go with this either. We make it to one of the beds, of course, mostly undressed.

The instant before he touched my arm, I wanted A.B.C. so much I'd have paid him to take me. Now that we're into it, I want him less and less. At first I don't understand it. It's because this is too sudden. Dancing those few times back in college is the closest we've been in the thirty years we've been acquainted. Now we're nearly naked, and it's a shock. What I thought I would like I don't like. I don't like his thumbs so insistently brushing my nipples. I don't like how his neck smells up in that hollow just below his ear, the place I've thought I would so dearly like to kiss. I don't like how he pushes his hips up between my thighs and keeps on pushing as if this were just the thing I should want him to do. I'm ashamed that my feelings are traitors like this. I'm trying to get myself to say something because A.B.C. is a train going down a mountain. Desire has been building up in me, too, all this time, so that my body is still moving with it even though I'm aware of how it's starting to pull back from what's happening. But A.B.C. is—

This monstrous noise rips itself up out of my throat, but it sounds like it's coming out of A.B.C. It's as if, suspended over me like this, he has taken control of my voice. Then I understand it. He shouted; I wailed—it was one sound. I'm also understand-ing that I'm crying now. A.B.C. gets that, too. He freezes. He's locked into me.

"What's wrong, U.?"

I can't tell him.

"Did I hurt you?"

I can at least shake my head. But then I'm nodding, too. I don't know what I'm telling him. I pull away from him. For a moment I don't think he's going to let me, but then he does. It hurts when he goes out of me. I turn my back to him and curl up. My shoulders are shaking. I want to be covered—being naked is what's hurting me now—but it's too crazy to try to get up and fix the bed covers over me. A.B.C. curls himself around me and tries to comfort me with his body. I know he's trying to make me feel better, but I don't want him here with me like this. I shake my head. He must get it because he moves away from me. In a second I feel a cover softly coming down over me. He's taken the spread from the other bed and brought it over to me.

That's when the phone rings.

It goes on ringing. I get myself to stop crying, but I don't move. A.B.C. doesn't either. He sits behind me, on the bed beside the table; I don't see him, but I know he's staring at the ringing phone. We don't move until it stops on maybe the tenth or twelfth ring. When the room is silent again, he says, "He's going to call back, U. You better get ready to talk to him."

I make myself sit up in the bed.

"You want the light on?" he asks.

I shake my head. Talking is completely out of the question. I pull this bedspread around me because I'm shivering.

Still naked, A.B.C. stands up and walks over to the window. First he peeks around the edge of the curtains. Then he opens them—and snaps us into another dimension. The room fills with this dark-yellow light from the outside. Huge flakes are still drifting down out there between the window glass and the black sky. This is what I've needed to see. I don't know how to explain it, but the snow coming down out there is as calming to me as when I was a kid sick in bed at night and my mother tiptoed into my room and brushed her hand across my forehead. I turn around on the bed and sit there watching the flakes sift down. A.B.C. watches them, too. We're held in a spell.

When the phone rings again, I pick it up right away. "Hey, Jimmy," I say. "I thought that was you just now. I just got out of the shower." My voice is fine. And because he doesn't question me, that about getting out of the shower is the only lie I have to tell him. He just wants to chat. The girls are still over at the Crandalls' house. He's feeling lonely at home by himself. Poor Jimmy, I feel so sentimental about him that I have lots more to say to him than I would have ordinarily. I tell him about the snow and the food A.B.C. and I had for dinner. I can see Jimmy sitting in our den with a basketball game on the TV, the sound muted, and a bottle of beer on the table beside him. While he's talking with me and watching the game, he's pushing his hand back through his hair. I know him so well that right then even his smallest habits seem very dear to me. I want to tell him what's happened to me and A.B.C. I want to tell him not so much because I feel guilty—though maybe that's what I do feel and just don't realize it—but because Jimmy and Marcy are the only two people in the world who could help me figure out what to make of it.

Of course they're the two I can't ever tell.

Jimmy had a sister—Edna—who died of leukemia when they were children. He was nine. She was seven. Edna with her huge eyes and her pale, bony face is this presence in our lives. Even the kids still ask him questions about her.

When it became clear what was wrong with Edna, the family let their doctor tell her everything, including that she was going to die. This doctor was a maverick back then in advocating that even little kids be told exactly what was happening to them. "Everybody needs to know the news," he said. "When the news is bad, the person needs it maybe even more than when it's good."

Jimmy said his sister took it in a funny way. Or maybe she took it in the right way, he wasn't sure. It was a neutral thing to her. Just a new fact she needed to get used to. If she was sad or scared, she never showed it. But she wasn't cheerful, either. Jimmy said it seemed to him that she took it on like a project for school, something she had to get done and handed in. She wanted a timetable. The only thing she ever complained about was that they couldn't seem to tell her exactly when she was going to die. She thought they ought to have it down to the hour. Even at the very end she was asking questions about that, about how much time she had left.

Edna became the family director. She especially liked parties, parties for kids her age, kids Jimmy's age, even parties for the grown-ups. She liked planning these parties and deciding things at them. "Now it's time to bob for apples," she'd say. Or, "Now I think we should all go into the living room for our dessert." Even when she couldn't really take part in games or eat very much, she liked to be there, liked making those decisions, liked seeing people do what she thought would make them happy.

The family got used to it. Mr. Rago checked with Edna every morning about what time she wanted him to be home from work. Mrs. Rago consulted with Edna about dinner menus for the week. Jimmy said it was weird, but he even got so he'd ask his little sister if he could have a friend over from school. He said Edna was very serious about the job, and she wasn't bad at it. Mostly she kept track of who was doing what and when, and she worked out decent schedules for everybody. He said it kept the rest of them cheered up. Even when she started going downhill the last time, and they all knew it was coming, as long as she could tell them something she wanted done, they felt like they could face whatever came next. "Edna says she wants these flowers over on that table," Mrs. Rago would whisper from Edna's bedside, and all three of them would be reaching for the vase of flowers.

We know this is a sentimental story. It doesn't matter. We don't tell it to anybody outside our family. Jimmy doesn't usually bring it up on his own, but sometimes I will know that he needs to tell some of it. Or I or one of the girls will need him to tell some of it.

"Would Edna tell you what clothes to wear?" I'll ask him. Then he'll have to think about that and try to remember. He'll start talking about her. The best is when he remembers something he hasn't told us before. The girls and I can get pretty excited when Jimmy tells us a new part of the Edna story. There was a famous haircutting that he came up with where Edna had this young man who came to her hospital room and did up her little tufts of white-blonde hair so that she looked strange and beautiful at the same time. I know it's childish of me, but I loved that new Edna chapter as much as any birthday or Christmas present I ever got.

The story of Edna has been going on since right after Jimmy and I got so caught up in each other in Charlottesville. We were taking a slow walk on the lawn on a sunny afternoon in April. Jimmy had his arm around my shoulder, and I had mine around his waist, because that's how we were with each other in those days. In this voice that was like humming a tune he wanted me to learn, he told me about his sister.

The thought occurred to me so suddenly that I had to interrupt him: "Have you ever told A.B.C. about Edna?"

Jimmy stopped walking and looked at me with the most horrified expression on his face. "You think I'd tell that guy that story?" he asked me. "Not in a million years," he said.

What he said felt just so right to me. Now and then over the span of our lives together I've had to ask him the same question again. We've never talked about what it means.

"Have you told him yet?" I'll ask.

"Told who what?" Jimmy will ask.

"A.B.C.," I'll say. "About Edna."

"No way," he'll say. "He doesn't get that story."

Then it seems like we can go on from there.

The Last Pages

JAMIE WEISMAN

*T*he dog in "Otto" is inspired by my own dog, Roy. As you can see, Roy is very large. He is a Bernese mountain dog, bred to pull cheese carts in the Swiss Alps. He doesn't do much cart pulling in Atlanta, but he does pull the kids in my neighborhood on their roller blades, which makes him very popular. Like Otto, he is gentle and sweet and very fond of ice cream. However, I am pleased to say that he was not given to me by anyone like Jeremy, but rather inherited from a friend when she moved back to the city from the country. I have known Roy since he was a puppy, and he has helped me through some tough times and some difficult transitions, as the dog in the story helps Hannah.

photo credit Victor Balaban

JANE ROSENZWEIG

I think my story "The End of the Decade" is about the ways people manage the past. I have always been intrigued by people who don't save anything, who seem to actively shed tangible evidence of their experiences. But I am equally fascinated by a more familiar impulse, the one that leads us to hold on to the material components of our lives as if the sum of these parts will somehow keep us whole. My closet is packed with boxes of old letters, ticket stubs, play programs, party invitations—fragments of my past that I can't bring myself to throw away. I am not convinced that I won't need these things, someday.

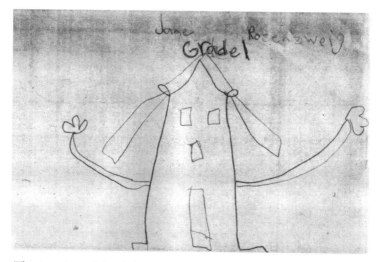

This is a picture I drew when I was in elementary school. My parents saved most of my drawings.

arion Ettlinger took this picture
of Bess, Molly, and me on a day when the lilac bush
in our backyard was blooming. Maybe we look this way
because the air was full of the fragrance of lilacs. Or maybe
Marion knew the right words to say just before she snapped the
picture. At any rate, there's a truth here that I cherish.

One of my pet theories about writing is that it depends on
one's capacity to continue learning. My daughters have demanded a certain alertness from me. I've had to keep on learning,
whether I wanted to or not; the bonus is that I've been able to
go on writing.

photo credit Marion Ettlinger

EUGENIE DOYLE

R ed Flag" is dedicated to my daughter, Nora, who is now eleven. After we sold our milking herd in 1992, I was tucking her into bed one night and confided sadly that I didn't know what I would do now, for work.

She said, "What did you dream of doing, when you were a little girl?"

My daughter with her Jobena.

An Olympic swimmer, a missionary, a veterinarian, a ballerina, a writer. That was my list.

"Then why are you a farmer?" she asked.

"Because I met Daddy and learned to love it."

"Well," she said, "now you can go back to Plan A."

We decided that, of the choices on my list, "writer" made most sense.

I'm glad my first published story is, in part, a salute to the foolish hopes rendered sensible by our children.

As I was racing out to mail this, a friend raced in and handed me these sketches.

ELLEN GILCHRIST

*D*esecration" is part of a collection for 1996 called *The Wraacks of Time*, a marvelous phrase I found in the *Episcopal Prayer Book* while enduring a terrible sermon. I had promised that if the University of Arkansas basketball team won the semifinals of the NCAA tournament last year I would attend the eleven o'clock service of the Episcopal church wearing a dress, pantyhose, and high-heeled shoes. I swore I would not resent being there. I promised I would take communion even though it terrifies me to drink from a communal cup. So there I was. I had sworn not to resent the morning, but I hadn't sworn not to read the hymnal to pass the time.

This story is very dear to me as I love Aurora Harris more than I have loved a character in many years. I ache and yearn for her and want to get her out of junior high as fast as possible before they ruin her forever. I do not need to tell my wonderful and brilliant readers that the desecration has nothing to do with what is going on on the altar.

Did I mention I'm a Pisces, not that I believe in horoscopes —

photo credit Don House

ROBERT COHEN

"The Boys at Night" was a found object, in a sense. The premise was just handed to me by an old friend whose sister and brother-in-law were being torn apart by a baby with Down's syndrome. I was twenty-five and single at the time; the trajectories of family life seemed as warpy and distant as space travel. But I knew at once how to write the story. I knew its shape, I knew its perspective, I knew the shades of rage and befuddlement that characterized its voice. I knew so much about it that I hardly felt the need to write it at all. Clearly all I needed to do was step back and let it get busy writing itself.

As it happened, the story did not write itself. *I* didn't write it either, not very well, though I tried and tried. It turned out that knowing so much at once about how to write the story was not a good thing at all. It slowed me down, screwed me up, made me blockish and slow. In the end it took about ten years (off and on) to hammer it into shape, such as it is. And even now the warped boards are groaning.

$\mathscr{P}$AST CONTRIBUTING AUTHORS AND ARTISTS
Issues 1 through 17 are available for eleven dollars each.

Robert H. Abel • Steve Adams • Susan Alenick • Rosemary Altea • A. Manette Ansay • Margaret Atwood • Brad Barkley • Kyle Ann Bates • Richard Bausch • Robert Bausch • Charles Baxter • Ann Beattie • Barbara Bechtold • Cathie Beck • Melanie Bishop • Corinne Demas Bliss • Valerie Block • Harold Brodkey • Danit Brown • Paul Brownfield • Evan Burton • Gerard Byrne • Jack Cady • Annie Callan • Kevin Canty • Peter Carey • Carolyn Chute • George Clark • Dennis Clemmens • Evan S. Connell • Tiziana di Marina • Stephen Dixon • Michael Dorris • Siobhan Dowd • Mary Ellis • James English • Tony Eprile • Louise Erdrich • Zoë Evamy • Michael Frank • Pete Fromm • Daniel Gabriel • Ernest Gaines • Tess Gallagher • Louis Gallo • Kent Gardien • Ellen Gilchrist • Peter Gordon • Elizabeth Graver • Paul Griner • Elizabeth Logan Harris • Marina Harris • Daniel Hayes • David Haynes • Ursula Hegi • Andee Hochman • Jack Holland • Lucy Honig • Linda Hornbuckle • David Huddle • Stewart David Ikeda • Lawson Fusao Inada • Elizabeth Inness-Brown • Andrea Jeyaveeran • Charles Johnson • Wayne Johnson • Elizabeth Judd • Jiri Kajanë • Hester Kaplan • Wayne Karlin • Thomas E. Kennedy • Lily King • Maina wa Kinyatti • Marilyn Krysl • Frances Kuffel • Anatoly Kurchatkin • Victoria Lancelotta • Jon Leon • Doris Lessing • Janice Levy • Christine Liotta • Rosina Lippi-Green • David Long • Salvatore Diego Lopez • William Luvaas • Jeff MacNelly • R. Kevin Maler • Lee Martin • Eileen McGuire • Gregory McNamee • Frank Michel • Alyce Miller • Katherine Min • Mary McGarry Morris • Bernard Mulligan • Abdelrahman Munif • Sigrid Nunez • Joyce Carol Oates • Tim O'Brien • Vana O'Brien • Mary O'Dell • Elizabeth Oness • Peter Parsons • Annie Proulx • Jonathan Raban • George Rabasa • Paul Rawlins • Nancy Reisman • Anne Rice • Roxana Robinson • Stan Rogal • Frank Ronan • Elizabeth Rosen • Janice Rosenberg • Kiran Kaur Saini • Libby Schmais • Natalie Schoen • Amy Selwyn • Bob Shacochis • Evelyn Sharenov • Floyd Skloot • Lara Stapleton • Barbara Stevens • William Styron • Liz Szabla • Paul Theroux • Patrick Tierney • Abigail Thomas • Randolph Thomas • Joyce Thompson • Andrew Toos • Patricia Traxler • Christine Turner • Kathleen Tyau • Michael Upchurch • Daniel Wallace • Ed Weyhing • Lex Williford • Gary Wilson • Terry Wolverton • Monica Wood • Christopher Woods • Celia Wren • Jane Zwinger.

B MULLIGAN

It's ready to fly!

There is a certain way that aunts raise their nieces and nephews. They love them for their missing sister, the dead, ill, or indifferent. A double love. Love for a ghost and then some.

from "The Lowest Blue Flame before Nothing"
by Lara Stapleton

Anyway, here was my dilemma: there was a dead husband on my back stairs and he wasn't mine.

from "Herb's Pajamas" by Abigail Thomas

The darkness that has settled over him, enveloped him, has become his constant and most intimate companion. In general, he has learned to accommodate himself to it.

from "A Middle-Aged Man" by Gary Wilson

When I had epilepsy, I would go off in these fugues, and I actually did end up in India one time, didn't know how I got there. I had a hotel key; I didn't know what hotel, and I was in India and it wasn't really funny. I didn't know how I got there, it was the strangest thing, and then it slowly came back to me.

from an interview with Thom Jones by Jim Schumock